PUFFIN BOOKS

BUMFACE

Morris Gleitzman was born and educated in England. He went to Australia with his family in 1969 and studied for a degree. In 1974 he began work with the ABC, left to become a full-time film and television writer in 1978 and has written numerous television scripts. He has two children and lives in Melbourne, but visits England regularly. Now one of the best-selling children's authors in Australia, his first children's book was *The Other Facts of Life*, based on his award-winning screenplay. This was followed by the highly acclaimed *Two Weeks with the Queen*, and he has since written many other books for children including *Toad Rage, Bumface,* and *Totally Wicked!* and *Deadly!* with Paul Jennings.

Visit Morris at his website:

BUMFACE

PUFFIN

For Angus

PUFFIN BOOKS

Published by the Penguin Group
Penguin Books Ltd, 80 Strand, London WC2R 0RL, England
Penguin Putnam Inc., 375 Hudson Street, New York, New York 10014, USA
Penguin Books Australia Ltd, 250 Camberwell Road, Camberwell, Victoria 3124, Australia
Penguin Books Canada Ltd, 10 Alcorn Avenue, Toronto, Ontario, Canada M4V 3B2
Penguin Books India (P) Ltd, 11 Community Centre, Panchsheel Park, New Delhi – 110 017, India
Penguin Books (NZ) Ltd, Cnr Rosedale and Airborne Roads, Albany, Auckland, New Zealand
Penguin Books (South Africa) (Pty) Ltd, 24 Sturdee Avenue, Rosebank 2196, South Africa

Penguin Books Ltd, Registered Offices: 80 Strand, London WC2R 0RL, England

www.penguin.com

First published in Australia by Penguin Books Australia Ltd 1998
Published in Puffin Books 1999

17

British Library Cataloguing in Publication Data
A CIP catalogue record for this book is available from the British Library

ISBN 0–141–30355–7

Part One

1

'Angus Solomon,' sighed Ms Lowry. 'Is that a penis you've drawn in your exercise book?'

Angus jumped, startled, and remembered where he was.

Ms Lowry was standing next to his desk, staring down at the page. Other kids were sniggering.

Angus felt his mouth go dry and his heart speed up. For a second he thought about lying. He decided not to.

'No, Miss,' he admitted, 'it's a submarine.'

Ms Lowry nodded grimly. 'I thought as much,' she said. 'Now stop wasting time and draw a penis like I asked you to.' She pointed to the one she'd drawn on the blackboard.

That's not fair, thought Angus. I wasn't wasting time.

He took a deep breath.

'Excuse me, Miss,' he said, 'I wasn't wasting

time. I was working on my pirate character for the school play. He lives in a submarine and –'

'Enough,' interrupted Ms Lowry. 'You know perfectly well play rehearsals aren't till tomorrow. Today we're doing human reproduction. I don't want to hear another word about pirates.'

Angus sighed as Ms Lowry turned away. I bet pirates don't let themselves be treated unjustly by teachers, he thought. I bet pirates stand up for themselves. I bet pirates have got really good lawyers.

He felt something prod his arm. It was Scott Mayo's ruler.

'Russell Hinch reckons you've called your pirate character Bunface,' whispered Scott. 'Is that right?'

'Bumface,' whispered Angus. 'His name's Bumface.'

'Angus Solomon,' yelled Ms Lowry. 'What did you just say?'

Trembling, Angus wondered if he could explain without dobbing in Scott.

He couldn't.

'B-Bumface,' he stammered.

A gasp ran through the class. Ms Lowry looked stunned. Oh no, thought Angus, horrified, she thinks I mean her.

'Not you,' he said hurriedly. 'My pirate.'

Ms Lowry took a very deep breath. Her eyes

narrowed and she looked dangerously stressed. Angus wondered if he should suggest she loosen the collar of her blouse. He decided not to risk it.

'You have five minutes to get this diagram into your book,' said Ms Lowry very quietly. 'If I hear another word about pirates before tomorrow, Angus Solomon, you're out of the school play.'

Angus tried to keep his mind on sex.

It wasn't easy. While Ms Lowry was busy telling off a kid up the front for putting a face on a testicle, Russell Hinch started getting laughs from his mates by showing them what he'd drawn in his exercise book. Angus caught a glimpse and felt his face go bright red.

Two figures, hand in hand.

Angus knew what they were meant to be even before he heard Russell's whisper.

'Angus Solomon and his girlfriend.'

Angus's cheeks burned and his insides sank.

Not again.

Not more joking and sniggering behind his back. Not more rumours spreading round the playground quicker than head lice. Rumours that were completely, totally, one million per cent untrue.

Angus pretended he hadn't heard. He pretended to be interested in Ms Lowry's diagram of the human reproductive organs on the blackboard.

Sex, he thought angrily. Sex, sex, sex. It's all we do in class these days. Why can't we do something interesting like geography?

Then he heard quiet sobs coming from behind him. He turned round. Stacy Kruger's face was crumpled and tears were dripping onto her exercise book. She looked so upset Angus couldn't help feeling sorry for her, even though she was always flicking things at him.

He leant back to speak to her, then stopped.

Russell Hinch and his mates were watching.

That's all I need, thought Angus. Russell Hinch spreading rumours I've got two girlfriends.

Angus reminded himself that talking to girls wasn't something he should be doing anyway. Not now he'd been given one of the main parts in the school play. Tough, ruthless, professional pirates didn't talk to girls. The audience wouldn't believe he was a pirate for a second if they knew he'd been talking to girls.

He looked at Stacy again. Her face was a wet mask of misery. Poor thing. He knew how she felt. He'd felt pretty weird himself the first time he'd found out what people had to do to make babies.

'It's OK,' he whispered to Stacy. 'Grown-ups like it.'

Stacy didn't seem to hear him. She sobbed some more.

'It doesn't hurt them or anything,' Angus whispered. 'My mum's always doing it.'

'Angus and Stacy,' yelled Ms Lowry, 'what is going on?'

Angus blushed and pretended he'd dropped his pencil.

'It's my baby,' sobbed Stacy. 'Someone's taken it.'

Angus stared at her. So did Ms Lowry.

'Your baby?' said Ms Lowry.

'I didn't know he was missing till just now,' sobbed Stacy. 'His beeper should have gone off and when it didn't I opened my pencil case and he wasn't there.'

Angus held his breath, waiting for Ms Lowry to explode.

'Stacy,' said Ms Lowry quietly. 'Are you talking about a Tamagotchi?'

Stacy nodded. 'If it doesn't get fed, it'll die,' she sobbed. 'And its battery could run out.'

Miss Lowry exploded. 'I've just about had it with this class today,' she yelled. 'Who took Stacy's Tamagotchi?'

Nobody spoke.

Angus looked around. Nobody looked guilty, not even Renee Stokes and Julie Cheng, who'd been going on for weeks about how they wished they had one.

'Right,' shouted Ms Lowry. 'Everyone outside for a bag search.'

7

Angus blinked. A bag search? For a Tama-gotchi? Kids weren't even meant to bring Tamagotchis to school.

Angus hoped he'd heard wrong.

He hadn't. The other kids were heading out to the pegs.

Fear stabbed through him. Not bags. Please not bags.

He hurried after Ms Lowry. 'Shouldn't we do pockets first?' he asked desperately.

'Pockets *and* bags,' snapped Ms Lowry.

Angus's insides sank lower than a submarine.

Angus stood miserably by his peg and prayed that the Tamagotchi would turn up before Ms Lowry got to his bag.

For a heart-stopping second he thought he saw it when Renee Stokes emptied out her bag, but it was just a plastic pencil-sharpener.

Then he thought he spotted it among the supermarket trolley wheels Russell Hinch tipped out of his bag, but it was just a box of matches.

'Last but not least,' said Ms Lowry, 'Angus Solomon.'

For a desperate moment Angus thought of telling her that his bag zip wouldn't open because it had been struck by lightning. Then he remembered lightning didn't strike indoors.

Only disasters did.

Angus emptied out his bag.

He watched Ms Lowry as she studied his things on the floor. She breathed an exasperated blast of air through her teeth when she saw the Tamagotchi wasn't there.

Stacy gave a sob and her face crumpled again.

Angus didn't even bother looking at Russell Hinch's face. He knew exactly what expression would be on it. As Russell stared gleefully at what *was* there.

A fluffy pink teddy with a yellow bow round its neck.

'Aw, sweet. Bumface has got a prezzie for his girlfriend.'

Face burning, Angus tried to ignore him.

I'm on a pirate submarine, he thought, at the bottom of the deepest part of that really remote bit of ocean the other side of Tasmania.

But even there he could still hear kids sniggering.

Angus sprinted across the playground, looking frantically at his watch.

Teachers shouldn't be allowed to have bag searches so close to the bell, he thought bitterly, not when people have to pick up younger brothers.

Leo was sitting by the infants gate, poking at something in the dust.

'Sorry I'm late,' panted Angus. 'You OK?'

Leo looked up and grinned. 'This spider just did a poo,' he shouted.

Angus sighed. Why did five-year-old boys have to be so loud?

'Leo,' he muttered, crouching, 'how would you like it if spiders went round yelling when you did a poo?'

Leo looked up at Angus, hurt. 'You told me to always tell the truth.'

Angus pulled him to his feet and dusted him off.

'I also told you something about spiders, didn't I?'

'They've got eight legs,' said Leo, 'and they don't eat fish.'

Angus grinned and gave Leo a hug. 'I told you not to touch them,' he said, picking bits of fruit out of Leo's hair, 'because some of them are poisonous and if they bite you you'll turn black. Though that seems to be happening already.'

He brushed dust off Leo's neck. How did five-year-old boys get so dirty?

'You told me I have to be brave,' said Leo. 'That's why I touch them.'

Angus sighed.

'Hey, Bumface, whatcha doin'?'

Angus turned. Russell Hinch stood grinning with a gang of kids. Scott was with them.

'We're going down the playground for some

pirate practice,' said Scott. 'Wanna come?'

'Thanks,' said Angus, 'but I can't.'

Russell nudged Scott. 'Told you,' he grinned. 'Bumface has got a date.' Scott grinned too. Russell turned to Angus. 'Hope your girlfriend likes her prezzie. She might give you one back.'

Angus watched Russell do his revolting kissy lips while the rest of them sniggered, including Scott.

Angus felt sick with unhappiness.

Suddenly he forgot he was meant to be setting a good example to Leo. He went over and stood on tiptoe and stuck his face close to Russell's. Russell looked startled.

'Listen, Dumbo,' said Angus. 'There's no girl, right? I'm not going to meet a girl. I'm not going to kiss a girl. Watch my lips. NO . . . GIRL . . .'

Panting, he glared at Russell, who took a nervous step back.

'Yes there is,' said Leo.

Russell and the others stared at Leo, then fell about.

Angus watched them laughing, his heart thumping and eyes pricking. He opened his mouth to explain, then closed it again. Instead he grabbed Leo and marched him away down the street.

'Ask her to lend you a dress for the school play,' yelled Russell.

Scott and the other kids chortled and Russell made kissy noises. Angus walked on, trying not to listen but hearing every smooch.

Leo looked up at him.

'I told the truth,' he whispered, 'like you said.'

'Yes,' said Angus sadly, 'you did.'

Leo squeezed Angus's hand. 'You were brave,' he said.

'Thanks,' said Angus with a sigh.

He wished he was brave enough to tell the truth himself. The truth about his life. But only little kids were that brave.

2

Imogen threw her arms round Angus and gave him a big wet kiss.

Angus glowed with pleasure, even though people were watching and he was pretty sure Imogen had jam on her mouth.

She pulled her lips away. Angus reached down and stroked her hair, then wiped the dribble and jam off his knee.

Imogen threw her arms round his other leg and kissed his other knee. 'Bumface,' she yelled happily.

Angus glanced anxiously at the other parents and crouched down. 'Imogen,' he whispered. 'Please try to remember. My name's not Bumface, it's Angus, right?'

'Bumface Gussy,' yelled Imogen, grinning.

Angus sighed. Oh well, he thought, you can't really blame her. There probably aren't many one-and-a-half-year-olds who've thought up a whole pirate name on their own. She's probably proud.

Imogen was frowning. 'Cindy,' she said.

Angus reached into his bag and pulled out Sidney the bear.

'Cindy,' squealed Imogen delightedly. Angus grinned as she buried her face in the pink fur.

She waddled out to the sandpit to show her friends. Angus was about to go after her when he noticed what Leo was doing. He raced over to the fish tank and grabbed Leo's wrist.

'We're not here to play,' said Angus. 'We're here to pick Imogen up. Anyway, fish don't eat crayons. Mrs Bennett gets very cross if people feed crayons to the fish.'

'No she doesn't,' said Leo. 'Mrs Bennett never gets cross. That's why it's called the Happy Family Childcare Centre.'

Angus was about to explain that Happy Family was a registered business name like Nintendo when Mrs Bennett's voice rang out across the exercise mats.

'Angus,' she said, 'can I have a little word?'

Angus prised the crayon from Leo's hand and stuffed it in his pocket.

'Ow,' protested Leo.

'Angus,' said Mrs Bennett, coming over, 'you're such a little trooper, dropping your sister off and picking her up each day. I wonder if I can give you one more little job.'

'No,' said Leo. 'He hasn't got time.'

Angus put his hand over Leo's mouth.

'What is it?' he said to Mrs Bennett.

'I am a bit concerned,' said Mrs Bennett, 'that we haven't seen your dad for a few weeks. Your mum did say that he'd be picking Imogen up most of the time himself.'

Angus's mouth was suddenly dry. He desperately tried to think of something to say.

'Dad's been very busy,' he blurted out.

That sounded OK.

'I'd feel happier if I had a quick word with your mum,' said Mrs Bennett. 'Could you ask her to give me a call? I've left several messages on her machine, but she hasn't got back to me.'

'No problem,' said Angus, trying to swallow. 'I'll tell her and . . . um . . . she'll get back to you.'

Angus didn't take his hand off Leo's mouth, just in case Leo told the truth again.

Angus looked anxiously at Imogen's nappy.

Almost full.

Why is it with one-and-a-half-year-olds, Angus thought wearily, that so much more comes out than you put in?

He calculated how far it was to home. Ten minutes at least. Keep absorbing, he begged the absorbent fibres in the nappy. He pushed the stroller faster along the bumpy footpath.

'Wheee,' shouted Imogen.

'Wait for me,' shouted Leo. 'I've got a ladybug that's eating an ant.'

'Keep up,' Angus panted.

He gave the bulging nappy another worried glance and thought about taking the quick route through the shopping mall. No. Too risky. Too many people could see them and ask awkward questions.

Keep expanding, he begged the expanding gussets.

'Look, the ladybug's eating chewing gum,' said Leo excitedly, trotting alongside. 'Well, chewing it.'

Angus swung the stroller round a corner and started to give Leo a lecture on the perils of picking things up in the street and encouraging insects to eat them.

Then he stopped, heart suddenly racing. Up ahead, jumping off a wall into the rubbish skip behind the supermarket, was the last person in the world he wanted to bump into.

Angus shoved the stroller behind a parked van and crouched down out of sight as Russell Hinch gave a bloodcurdling pirate yell.

'There's your friends,' said Leo. 'Shall I tell them we're playing hide and seek?'

Angus grabbed him. 'They mustn't see us,' whispered Angus.

'Why not?' said Leo.

Angus was tempted to try and explain. About how if the other kids found out about Mum, soon the whole school would know, then the suburb, then the next suburb, then the whole of Australia.

No. What would happen then was too scary for a little kid.

'You're too young to understand,' whispered Angus. 'I'll explain when you're older.'

'You'll forget by then,' said Leo.

Imogen's nappy rumbled. Angus wished he'd packed a spare one in his school bag. Then he remembered the bag search and was glad he hadn't.

He peered round the back of the van and watched Russell Hinch give another pirate yell and run off towards the mall followed by Scott and the others.

That's what happens when people haven't got any family responsibilities, thought Angus. They get chucked out of playgrounds and mistreat rubbish containers and make too much noise and spend hours and hours thinking up really good pirate characters for the school play.

'I wish we could go with them,' said Leo. 'We could if we pretended to be pirates.'

Little kids, thought Angus wearily as he steered Leo and Imogen home.

They never give up.

*

'I want Mummy,' wailed Imogen.

'Me too,' shouted Leo.

Angus put the saucepan and the potato-masher down, wiped his hands on his apron and went out to the living room. He picked Imogen up and gave her a hug.

'Immie,' he said gently, 'you know that's not possible. Not now. Be a brave girl and let me finish making dinner.'

'What about me being a brave boy?' demanded Leo.

'You're a very brave boy,' said Angus.

'I don't want to be,' said Leo. 'I want Mummy.'

Angus sighed. Poor kids, he thought. Must be even harder for them than it is for me.

Then he realised his feet were wet. He looked down. All around him the carpet was sodden and covered in soap bubbles.

'You kicked the bucket over,' said Leo quietly.

Angus saw, near his feet, the yellow bucket from the laundry lying on its side with a last few soap bubbles dribbling onto the carpet.

'Hot,' said Imogen. Angus felt the inside of his head get hot too.

'What is this bucket doing in here?' he yelled, pulling his apron off and trying to mop up some of the water with it.

Imogen started to cry.

'Immie wanted to wash Sidney's hair,' said Leo.

'Cindy hair,' wailed Imogen.

Angus saw a sodden Sidney the bear lying next to the bucket. 'So you let her?' he yelled at Leo. 'You went to the laundry and filled a bucket with hot soapy water and brought it into the living room just because a one-and-a-half-year-old asked you to?'

'No,' said Leo indignantly. 'It was already in here. I was washing some ants.'

Angus smelt something burning. For a second he thought it was his brain. Then he realised it was the fish fingers.

Leo was crying as well now.

'I want Mummy,' sobbed Imogen.

'So do I,' wailed Leo.

Angus ran into the kitchen, pulled the fish fingers out of the grill, dropped his wet apron on them to stop them smoking, ran into the laundry, grabbed the mop, ran back into the living room, mopped up the water, wrung Sidney out into the bucket, opened the window so the carpet would dry, took everything back to the laundry and put Sidney in the dryer.

Then, out of breath, he looked at his watch.

Six-thirty.

At last.

Angus went back to the living room, wiped the tears off the kids' faces with his apron and gave them a hug each.

'Who wants to see Mummy?' he said.

'Me,' screeched Imogen.

'Me too,' yelled Leo.

'Well, you've come to the right place,' grinned Angus, 'because here's that very special person we've all been waiting for . . . Mummy.'

He switched on the TV.

3

During the first commercial break, Leo disappeared.

'Leo,' called Angus, 'you'll miss Mum.'

'I'm on the toilet,' came Leo's faint cry.

The commercial break ended and Mum appeared on the screen in her spotless TV living room hugging two of her spotless TV children.

Don't know why they call this series a soapie, thought Angus. They're all too clean to need soap.

On the screen Mum was giving her TV twins her famous warm, caring TV smile.

Angus felt the usual pang of jealousy and reminded himself that she was only acting.

Imogen jiggled excitedly in her high chair and pointed at the TV. 'Mama,' she yelled happily, spraying a mouthful of chocolate milk over the table.

'Immie,' said Angus quietly. 'Do you think

just tonight we could try to be as clean and tidy as Mummy's TV family?'

'Mama,' yelled Imogen again and threw a handful of mashed potato and pumpkin across the room.

Obviously not, thought Angus wearily.

'I'm missing Mum,' came Leo's distant yell.

'Well, hurry up,' called Angus.

'I can't,' yelled Leo. 'I'm stuck.'

Angus ran to the bathroom. Leo wasn't in there. Angus sprinted down to Mum's en suite, then heard Leo yelling in the guest toilet. He doubled back, desperately hoping Leo hadn't fallen into the dunny while he was flushing it.

The door of the guest toilet wouldn't open.

'The lock's stuck,' yelled Leo.

'Are you all right?' shouted Angus frantically. Leo always forgot to close his mouth under water. In a sewer pipe he'd be history.

'No, I'm not all right,' yelled Leo. 'I can't see Mum. What's she doing?'

Angus peered down the hall. On the TV in the living room Mum was still talking to the twins in her famous warm, caring TV voice. Angus heard Imogen gurgle 'Mama' and saw chocolate milk splatter over the screen.

'What's Mum doing?' yelled Leo.

Angus strained to hear.

'She's telling Lachlan and Courtney to stop worrying,' Angus shouted through the door.

'She's going to meet them after school and go to the newsagent's with them, and if Mr Green overcharges them for lollies again he'll be sorry.'

'What?' yelled Leo.

'Open the door,' yelled Angus. 'Try harder. Spit on the key.'

'What's Mum doing now?' yelled Leo.

From the living room Angus heard the splat of something hitting the wall.

'Never mind about Mum,' he yelled frantically. 'Immie's in there on her own with mashed pumpkin and chocolate milk and stewed fruit.'

Angus heard Leo spitting on the key.

'It's not working,' wailed Leo.

The lock needs more lubrication, thought Angus desperately. If Mum was home they could drain some oil out of her car, but she'd be taping at the studio for at least another hour. What if the TV people kept her really late for retakes and by the time she got home Leo had starved to death? He'd hardly touched his fish fingers.

Angus tried to bash the door in with his shoulder.

The door didn't budge. His shoulder hurt a lot.

Then Angus noticed a lump of mashed potato and pumpkin on the front of his school shirt. He scraped it off and stuffed it into the keyhole.

'Try now,' he shouted.

The key turned in the lock.

Angus pushed the door open and grabbed Leo and inspected him anxiously for signs of drowning or hysteria.

He couldn't see any.

'Are you all right?' he asked, relieved.

'No,' said Leo tearfully, 'Mum's on and I'm missing her.'

Leo ran back to the living room. Angus followed, wondering how old kids had to be before they thanked you for using lots of butter in the mashed potato and pumpkin.

Imogen was dripping with chocolate milk and smeared with mashed vegies and gazing happily at the food-spattered screen where Mum was having dinner in her spotless TV kitchen with her spotless TV family.

Angus looked around the real-life living room and nearly fainted.

The damp patch on the carpet suddenly didn't look so bad. Not compared to the tomato sauce running down the wall. And the stewed fruit splattered over Mum's awards. And the chocolate milk dripping off the indoor ferns. And the dollop of potato and pumpkin on the Prime Minister's head.

If the Prime Minister was here and saw this, thought Angus gloomily, he'd never have his photo taken with Mum at a charity lunch ever again.

Angus sat down and closed his eyes and wondered how he was going to clean it all up before Mum got home. Plus do the dishes, make Leo and Imogen's lunch for tomorrow, disinfect the stroller and do his human reproduction homework.

He felt panic starting to bubble up inside him.

He remembered what the lifestyle-show doctor Mum had gone out with last year had reckoned you should do about panic. Imagine you were in a beautiful place. The doctor had done several segments on panic, possibly because he'd been going out with Mum.

Angus tried to imagine he was floating in a pirate submarine through the Great Barrier Reef. He tried to see the dazzling coral and exotic fish through the gun sights. It was no good. He couldn't concentrate. Not with that horrible noise Leo was making.

Angus opened his eyes.

Leo was spitting out a mouthful of half-chewed fish finger.

'Leo,' said Angus, exasperated. 'I cut off most of the burnt bits.'

On the screen Mum's beaming TV husband Max was handing her a spotless TV plate. 'A slice of pizza for Australia's best mum,' he said.

In return she gave him one of her famous crinkly-nose TV kisses.

Angus winced. Watching her do that always made him feel funny in the tummy, though tonight it was probably made worse by stress and soggy burnt fish fingers.

'Not fair,' wailed Leo. 'Craig and Nolene and Lachlan and Courtney are having pizza. Why can't we have pizza?'

Angus took a deep breath. 'We've been through all this,' he said. 'They're Mum's TV family. They're not real. We're her real family. We're the lucky ones. Immie, don't put your dinner in your nappy.'

'We're not as lucky as them,' said Leo, reaching for the tomato sauce and knocking his orange cordial over. 'Mum spends heaps more time with them. They're luckier.'

'She has to spend more time with them,' said Angus. 'It's her job. It's how she earns the money we need to live on.'

'She's our mum,' said Leo tearfully. 'She should spend more time with us.'

Angus grabbed a kitchen sponge and started mopping up. He felt a chill running up his spine. It wasn't just the cordial soaking into his shirt. It was because Leo was right.

Angus wiped the feeling away.

Little kids, they were too young to understand.

*

Angus was still wiping pumpkin off the Prime Minister when Mum's show ended.

Please, begged Angus silently as Mum disappeared from the screen, don't go.

She went.

Imogen gave a howl of rage and threw a handful of stewed plums and pears at Mum's CD player. Angus managed to catch most of it.

Leo sulked.

As usual Angus cheered them both up by giving them a relaxing bath and making funny Bumface voices come out of Leo's plastic submarine. This kept them distracted while he washed the potato and pumpkin out of Imogen's belly button and the spider webs out of Leo's hair.

Angus noticed that Leo's right earlobe looked a bit pink and swollen. He wrapped both the kids in towels, then hurried into his room to check his books.

None of them had anything about swollen earlobes or spider bites. Angus couldn't believe it. How can people write parenting books, he thought bitterly, and leave out all the important stuff?

Angus went back into the bathroom, made Imogen spit out the soap, explained to Leo that toothpaste was not for painting expensive bottles of perfume with, then examined Leo's earlobe again and decided it was just a phase he was going through.

When the kids' teeth were brushed, Angus took them to say goodnight to Leo's mouse Geoffrey.

Angus looked into the cage and frowned. Geoffrey was looking very fat these days.

'What have you been feeding him?' asked Angus.

'Ants,' said Leo.

Angus peered at Geoffrey's swollen tummy. He must have eaten most of the ants in the district.

Angus tucked the kids into bed and told them a Bumface story. It was the one where Bumface kidnapped a whole bunch of parents and took them to his secret pirate submarine base on a remote island and kept them there until they promised to spend more time with their families.

Even though it was one of Imogen and Leo's favourites, they still had sad faces at the end.

'I want my dad,' said Leo.

Angus sighed. 'Your dad's busy, Leo,' he said gently. 'He works nights, remember?'

'My dad,' said Imogen.

'Your dad's busy too,' said Angus.

'Your dad's not busy,' Leo said to Angus, 'cause he's unemployed.'

Angus caught sight of his own weary face in Leo's mirror. 'A person can still be busy,' he said, 'even when they're not being paid.'

'When can they?' said Leo.

Angus thought about the sauce-spattered wall waiting for him, and the lunchboxes and the stroller and the homework.

He decided not to depress the little kids.

'When they're a pirate,' he yelled, and tickled them both.

They screamed with laughter.

Angus laughed too, and as he looked at their joyful faces he found himself wishing that a pirate would swing in through the bedroom window on a pirate rope and carry them all off to a secret pirate submarine base where they could always be like this.

One day, thought Angus.

It might happen.

4

Angus had just finished wiping the walls and was reaching into the dishwasher for Leo's lunchbox when he heard a high-pitched voice behind him.

'Avast there, me hearty.'

He looked round.

A cloth hand-puppet that looked sort of like a pirate was poking round the kitchen door.

'I'm Pirate Jim,' said the voice. 'Splice me mainbrace and always wash your hands before meals.'

'Hi Dad,' said Angus wearily.

Dad came in grinning broadly and waggling the pirate puppet on his hand. 'What do you reckon?' he said.

'Kids TV show?' asked Angus hopefully. Dad really needed a career break.

Dad frowned under his curls. 'That hopeless agent of mine couldn't get me a role in a bread shop,' he said, 'let alone a TV show.' Then he grinned again. 'So I'm not moping around waiting any more. I'm writing a kids book. *Pirate Jim*. I got the idea from you when you told me how you'd persuaded your teacher to do a school play about pirates.'

Angus stared at him. 'Dad,' he said, 'you're an actor, not a writer.'

'Loads of actors write when they're between jobs,' said Dad. 'Anyway, kids books are easy once you've got an idea. Mine's a corker. Pirate Jim's an ex-policeman who sails the world in an ecologically sound yacht telling bad kids how much more fun it is to be good. What do you think?'

Angus suddenly found it hard to look at Dad. 'Where did you get the puppet?' he said, rummaging around in the dishwasher for Imogen's lunchbox.

'I'm going out with someone who used to do puppet theatre,' said Dad. 'Before she got into aerobics.'

Angus sighed.

'Thing is,' said Dad, 'I need a bit of help with research. You're a good kid. What are your favourite fun things? The best things about being a kid? The things that make you glad to be alive?'

Angus thought for a long time. Dad didn't seem to notice because he and Pirate Jim were busy helping themselves to the chocolate biscuits.

'The school play,' said Angus.

Dad wrote that down in a notebook.

'And . . . ?' said Dad.

Angus was still struggling to think of something else when he heard the sound of Mum's car in the driveway.

'Actually,' said Dad, 'there is another reason I popped round. I need to borrow a bit of cash from Mum. Has she got any around the place?'

Angus's insides sank. 'Dad,' he said, 'Mum said no more. She pays you for child-minding and that's it.'

'Aw, come on,' said Dad. 'It's only till I do a deal with a publisher for the book.'

'I'm sorry,' said Angus, 'I can't.' His chest felt tight and numb. 'You'll have to ask her yourself.'

Outside, Mum's car door slammed.

'Some other time,' said Dad. 'I want to get home and get on with the book. Avast there me hearty and don't forget to eat your vegies.' He tweaked Angus's nose with Pirate Jim, winked a couple of times and headed for the back door.

Then he stopped and came back and gripped Angus's shoulders.

'Sorry I haven't been around much lately to help you with the kids after school,' he said hurriedly. 'I just can't afford the time. Your mum only pays me a pittance and I'm putting really long hours into *Pirate Jim*. Plus I have to pick Kelly up from aerobics. But you're coping OK, right?'

Angus didn't blink.

'Yes, Dad,' he said. 'Don't worry.'

Dad grinned. 'My Mr Reliable,' he said.

Angus glowed. He waited for a hug. But Dad just tweaked Angus's nose again and was gone.

Angus sighed and reminded himself that Dad was in a hurry.

He leant against the fridge. He saw that his hands were shaking. It's just exhaustion, he thought dully. It's my body's way of telling me it knows I haven't even started the kids' lunches for tomorrow.

Angus hoped Dad hadn't noticed any signs of exhaustion.

It was hard enough for a bloke to write a best-selling series of pirate books and save his career without having to worry about whether his son was suffering from a bit of tiredness.

Angus was laying out the bread for the kids' sandwiches when he heard Mum's bracelets jangling in the hallway. She came into the kitchen, dropped her bag and coat onto the floor, and threw her arms round him.

'You darling,' she said, hugging him to her chest, 'you're doing their lunchboxes. I don't know how I'd survive without you.'

Angus glowed. This was his favourite part of the day, even though he almost choked on the smell of the stuff she used to get her TV makeup off.

She pulled herself away and left him gasping for breath. Then he saw her face. It was creased with concern. She was staring at a magazine in her hand.

'What's wrong?' said Angus, his heart picking up speed.

'Nothing,' said Mum, going through to the living room. Angus hurried after her. She kicked her shoes off and flung herself onto the settee and flicked her hair out of her eyes and waved the magazine. 'Except I'll probably lose my job.'

Angus's heart stopped. He stared at her, clammy with panic.

It must have happened, the thing he'd feared most. A gossip magazine must have discovered the hours she worked and printed a story about Australia's favourite TV mum neglecting her own kids in real life.

Angus's head spun with horrible thoughts. The viewers wouldn't want to watch her any more, not if they thought she was a fake. The network would sack her. There'd be no money for food or rent or nappies . . .

I'll write to the magazine, thought Angus desperately. I'll explain the sort of hours TV soap actors have to work and how their families really don't mind except for husbands and little kids.

Angus's frantic eyes focused on the page Mum was staring at. Hang on, that photo wasn't of him cooking Leo and Imogen's dinner. It hadn't been taken by a journalist hiding outside the kitchen window in the compost bin. It was a shot of Mum at an Awards night with Number Four.

'. . . not fair,' Mum was saying. 'Just because two people work together, why shouldn't they have a relationship? Why should the media make it into some sort of scandal? Gavin's a single director, I'm a single actress, OK, a divorced actress, why shouldn't we fall in love? Why shouldn't I have a chance at fourth time lucky?'

Feeling crept back into Angus's body. A sort of giddy tingling. He swallowed and found his voice. 'Why will you probably lose your job?' he croaked. 'TV stars don't lose their jobs for being in love, do they?'

Mum ran her hand through her hair and grinned at him. 'No,' she said. 'I was just being dramatic. OK, the network doesn't like me being in magazine photos they haven't arranged, but I'll flutter my eyelashes at a few bosses and it'll be right.'

Angus leant against the table, weak with relief.

'Sorry if I scared you,' said Mum. 'You know I get carried away a bit sometimes. It's my emotional, creative, passionate nature. Where Gavin's concerned, I'm like a three-year-old with a new bike.'

She jumped up and hugged Angus again.

'Sorry I'm getting home so late these days,' she said. 'When I finish taping there's always more chores to do. Interviews. Autographs. Drinks with the sponsor. Still, at least you've got Dad to give you a hand. I know he's pretty hopeless, but his heart's in the right place. Are you sure you're coping OK, the two of you?'

Angus didn't blink.

'Yes, Mum,' he said. 'Don't worry.'

'I don't know what I'd do without you, Angus,' she said, kissing him on the head. 'My Mr Dependable.'

Angus glowed through his tiredness.

Mum went to say goodnight to Leo and Imogen.

Angus wandered wearily into the kitchen. As he picked up Mum's coat, he hoped Mum hadn't spotted any signs of exhaustion.

It was hard enough for a woman to be the star of a very demanding TV series and provide a roof over her family's head single-handed without having to worry about whether her son was suffering from a bit of fatigue.

Angus told himself not to fret. She wouldn't

have noticed anything. After all this time, one thing he was good at was pretending.

A thought hit him.

Of course. That's why the school play was so important to him. That's why it was the only part of his life where he could really have fun.

I'm the same as Mum, thought Angus with a weary smile.

I love acting.

5

Bumface swung across the deck of his submarine on a gym rope and, with a single blow of his flashing cutlass, sliced the top off a coconut.

Greedily he gulped down the sweet milk, not caring that half of it was splashing onto his pirate waistcoat. With a growl of satisfaction he threw the empty shell on the floor. Then he sliced the tops off the crew's coconuts and drank those too.

Let 'em go thirsty, he thought. Pack of hairy, lice-ridden thugs.

He threw the crew's empty coconuts on the floor, except for one with a bit of milk left in it which he saved for the ship's cat who'd been looking a bit under the weather lately. He wondered if she'd been injured in battle, or was possibly even pregnant.

'Come on, Angus,' yelled Ms Lowry across the school hall. 'Speed it up.'

Angus sighed. I bet Mel Gibson doesn't get interrupted like this in rehearsals, he thought. And I bet he gets a real cutlass and real coconuts to work with instead of having to mime everything.

Angus dived back into character and soon forgot that the bare school hall didn't look anything like a submarine.

Bumface grabbed a leg of roast beef, took a couple of big bites, tossed the rest into the sink with the dirty dishes, noticed the toast was burning, snatched it out of the toaster, scraped it with his cutlass, didn't even care that the burnt bits went all over the clean washing basket, smeared jam on with his fingers, decided he didn't feel like taking the crew to training school this morning, got back into his hammock with his boots on, and started daydreaming happily about making Russell Hinch walk the plank in his underwear.

'Angus,' yelled Ms Lowry, striding towards him across the stage. 'This scene is going on about a week too long.'

Angus blinked at her.

'It's a very simple scene,' said Ms Lowry, 'Bluebeard has breakfast before he goes into battle. I put it in to show how we need a nutritious start to the day.'

Angus sighed. How many times had he told her his name was Bumface? Even at the very beginning, when she'd announced that the school play was about history and geography and he'd asked if it could have pirates in it and she'd said yes, he'd told her his pirate was called Bumface.

This is what always happens, thought Angus gloomily. When a kid has an idea and tells it to a grown-up, the grown-up takes over.

He knew because he was always doing it to Leo.

'My name's Bumface,' said Angus quietly to Ms Lowry.

'No it is not,' said Ms Lowry. 'And I don't want to hear that word again.'

Angus opened his mouth to protest, then closed it. He reminded himself that sometimes adults had trouble imagining things.

Ms Lowry turned to the rest of the class. 'OK,' she said, 'I want to run through the battle scene to see if I'm going to need professional help to stage it. Positions everyone. Pirates this side, Xena and her army this side. And no hitting.'

Angus was just starting to really enjoy himself in the battle scene when Stacy Kruger sidled over.

'I know you've got it,' she hissed.

'Sorry?' panted Angus. He was in the middle of chopping a dishwasher to pieces with his cutlass.

'My Tamagotchi,' hissed Stacy. 'I know you took it.'

Angus stared at her, bewildered. Then hurt. How could she think that? 'No I didn't,' he said.

'I can prove you did,' said Stacy. 'I've got a witness.'

Angus was about to ask who when he saw Russell Hinch watching them both and smirking.

I should have guessed, thought Angus.

'Bluebeard,' yelled Ms Lowry. 'Don't just stand there, it's a battle. And Queen of Spain, you're not in this scene.'

Stacy stamped away, glaring at Angus.

Angus took a deep breath and decided not to let injustice ruin his rehearsal.

The battle was taking place in a market square in Constantinople. Bumface leapt into a frantic cutlass duel with an astronaut who'd arrived via a time-warp (Doug Fawcett). Then he was attacked from behind by one of Xena's hired assassins (Kevin Posser). They fought desperately across the marketplace, hurling rolls of cloth, burning kebabs, brass ornaments and lumps of dried goat meat at each other. Finally Bumface trapped the assassin in an ice-cream factory and overpowered him by putting lemon gelato in his loincloth.

'They didn't have lemon gelato in twelfth-century Constantinople,' complained Kevin.

'Doug brought it with him through the time-warp,' replied Angus happily.

Then he saw the Sultan's children being held hostage in a toilet and hurried over to rescue them.

By the time Ms Lowry called an end to the battle, Angus's face was glowing with perspiration and pleasure.

This is the best, he thought happily. And it'll be even better when we've got a script and costumes.

'That was a shambles,' said Ms Lowry. Her shoulders slumped and she massaged her eye sockets with the palms of her hands. 'I'm going to need some help to get this play on,' she muttered. 'I knew when Mr Arnott couldn't do it this year I shouldn't have volunteered on my own.'

Angus saw the assassins starting to look panicked, like little kids whose mum had just announced she couldn't cope.

Angus was feeling a bit panicked himself. This was no time for Ms Lowry to be losing her nerve.

'I think you're doing a good job, Miss,' said Angus. 'For a first-timer you're doing a great job.'

'Yeah,' said most of the assassins enthusiastically. 'For a first-timer.'

'And you're a good class teacher, too,' said Angus.

'Crawler,' muttered Russell Hinch.

'All right, Angus,' said Ms Lowry. 'Don't push it. Now before we go back to class, I've got an important announcement. I've been talking to the principal about our rehearsal schedule.'

Good, thought Angus. They've realised three rehearsals a week aren't enough and we need five.

'The principal agrees with me,' continued Ms Lowry, 'that three rehearsals a week is too disruptive to our class work.'

What? thought Angus.

'So,' said Ms Lowry, picking up a pile of photocopies, 'here's a letter to notify your parents that from tomorrow rehearsals will be after school.'

Angus stared at her, horrified.

He struggled to speak.

'Please Miss, not after school.'

Ms Lowry gave him a long-suffering look.

'Some of us ...' said Angus, frantically trying to find the right words, '... some of us have to do things after school.'

'Ooooooh,' sang out Russell Hinch.

'Button it, Russell,' said Ms Lowry. 'Angus, if you've got a problem after school, I'm happy to discuss it.'

Angus felt his face burning hotter than a

Constantinople kebab stall. Everyone was looking at him. He didn't dare say anything. For all he knew any one of these kids' mums or dads could work for a magazine or a newspaper or the TV news. Any one of them could be itching to write a story about TV stars neglecting their kids.

'I think you're embarrassing him, Miss,' grinned Russell. He made kissy lips and the other kids sniggered.

'I know there might be some inconvenience,' said Ms Lowry, 'but I'm sure people who really want to be in the play will make the effort. Now, everyone back to class.'

Angus watched helplessly as she led the kids out of the hall. Then suddenly he sprinted after them.

In the corridor he grabbed Ms Lowry by the arm. 'Miss,' he blurted out, 'I need to speak to you privately.'

Ms Lowry sighed heavily and sent the class captain on ahead with the other kids. Angus took a deep breath and got ready to do his best acting.

'Yes?' said Ms Lowry.

'It's our local newsagent,' said Angus. 'He's been overcharging me for lollies. Me and Mum have to keep an eye on him each day after school to make sure he doesn't do it to other kids.'

Angus held his breath and desperately hoped

Ms Lowry hadn't seen that bit on Mum's show.

Ms Lowry's face darkened with anger.

Oh no. She had.

'I'm very disappointed in you, Angus,' said Ms Lowry. 'I know life can't always be easy for you, having such a famous mother, but I just don't understand your attitude these days. Is there a problem you haven't told me about?'

Angus saw a flicker of concern on her face. A voice inside him suddenly wanted to tell her everything.

Act, Angus told himself frantically. Act.

'No, Miss,' he said, trying to sound surprised at the very suggestion.

He watched the concern fade from Ms Lowry's face.

'Well, young man,' she said. 'I want to see an end to this childish behaviour. I suggest you start trying to be a bit more like your mother. A full-time job on national television and bringing up a family, I think she's amazing.'

Angus nodded helplessly.

'If you ever lie to me again,' said Ms Lowry, 'there will be serious consequences. What you need to do, young man, is grow up.'

Miserably, Angus kept on nodding.

Angus stared at the broccoli, deep in thought.

After-school rehearsals started in twenty-two

and a half hours. There had to be a way.

Behind him he heard Imogen knocking things off the supermarket shelf, followed by Leo's loud whisper.

'Imogen, not the panty pads.'

'Gussy panty pad,' shrieked Imogen.

'Angus doesn't want a panty pad,' whispered Leo. 'He's brooding.'

Angus sighed at the broccoli. If only he could leave Imogen an extra hour at the childcare centre on rehearsal days. But she got upset if he was ten minutes late. An hour and she'd be hysterical. Plus Mrs Bennett was starting to get suspicious about Mum. This afternoon she'd asked if she could ring Mum at work.

'Has Mummy abandoned you?' said a voice.

Angus jumped guiltily. A woman shopper was smiling down at him.

'Doing shopping for Mummy?' she asked.

Angus nodded.

'You look as though you need some help,' said the woman. 'This is broccoli. It's a green vegetable. You boil it in very hot water.'

'I've tried that,' said Angus. 'I've also steamed it with baby squash and stir-fried it with mushrooms and baked it with tomato and ricotta but the kids still won't eat it.'

Angus realised the woman was giving him a funny look. Behind her, next to the checkout, he could see a rack of the sort of magazines that dobbed in celebrity families who were careless and said too much.

'Thanks for the advice,' he said hurriedly.

The woman, still looking a bit stunned, wheeled her trolley away.

After she'd gone, Angus felt guilty he hadn't said thank you properly, because her advice had been spot on.

He did need help.

6

'Dad,' shouted Angus, 'I need help.'

Dad, who was trying to get bubble gum off Pirate Jim's moustache with an ice cube, didn't even hear him.

Angus wasn't surprised. It was hard to hear anything with a million little kids running around yelling.

He scooped Imogen up before she could get trampled, and had a closer look at the kids. There were actually only about six, but in Dad's little house that seemed like a million.

'Sorry about the racket,' said Dad. 'I asked some of the local kids in after school so I could do some Pirate Jim research, but things have got a bit out of control.'

He winced as a loud crash came from the other end of the living room.

'Avast there,' he called. 'Pirate Jim says shiver

me timbers and always look after other people's property.'

Angus watched as the kids ignored Dad and carried on having noisy fun.

Pack of delinquents, thought Angus. But he had to admit that if he wasn't feeling so sorry for Dad he might even be a bit jealous of them.

'Pirate Jim's mouth isn't working properly,' explained Dad. 'It's the bubble gum. I should never have let the kids hold him.'

Angus agreed he shouldn't.

'What were you saying just now?' asked Dad.

Angus tried to tell Dad about the school play and the rehearsals, but halfway through they both had to leap across the room and stop a bookcase with a kid on it from toppling over.

'Don't worry, Dad,' said Angus. 'I can see you've got your hands full and I've got to get Leo and Imogen home, so I'll say goodbye.'

Outside in the street Angus could still hear the faint sound of Dad's voice. 'Avast there,' he was saying. 'Splice me mainbrace and put that china fruit bowl down immediately.'

Leo tugged at Angus's hand.

'Is your dad gunna look after us while you go to rehearsals?' he said.

Angus shook his head. If poor old Dad

couldn't even control half a dozen seven-year-olds, he'd be completely out of his depth with Leo and Imogen.

Angus saw that Leo was looking concerned.

'Don't worry, Leo,' he said. 'Tomorrow afternoon we'll go and see your dad.'

The door chimes at Number Two's big terrace house played 'Jingle Bells'.

Angus realised he hadn't heard that since Number Two was married to Mum. Number Two must have got custody of the front door bell.

Angus heard Number Two coming down the hall singing along with the chimes. The hours I spent teaching him the words, thought Angus, and he still hasn't got them right.

Number Two opened the door and Angus saw his face fall, just for a second. Then Number Two gave Leo a big open-mouthed grin, just like he used to give the audience in *The Rocky Horror Show*.

'G'day, old mate,' he boomed. 'What are you doing here?'

'G'day, Dad,' said Leo. 'Angus brought us.'

Angus was halfway through rehearsing in his head what he planned to say when he realised Number Two was looking at him.

The grin was gone.

Angus took a deep breath. 'We're doing a

play at school,' he said, 'and Ms Lowry needs some professional help staging the battle scene and as you're one of the top stage actors in the country I thought I'd ask you.'

Number Two frowned while he took this in. Then he gave an even bigger grin than before. 'Be happy to,' he said. 'Get Ms Whatsername to give me a ring.'

'And,' continued Angus, 'I was wondering if you could mind Leo and Imogen for a few afternoons after school while I go to rehearsals.'

Number Two didn't say anything. His eyes narrowed. He gave Angus a hard look.

'Did your mother put you up to this?' he said.

'No,' said Leo. 'It was Angus's idea.'

'Gussy panty pad,' said Imogen.

'Mum's very busy,' said Angus quietly. 'I didn't want to bother her.'

'Very busy,' said Number Two. 'Can't be bothered. Yes, that sounds like your mother. Well I'm afraid I'm very busy too.'

Angus felt Leo's hand tighten around his.

'I'm sorry, Leo,' continued Number Two. 'I have to be at the theatre by six each evening and I spend at least two hours before that doing voice exercises. It's just not practical. But as soon as I get a chance, old mate, I'm going to take you to the zoo. Next month.'

'What about . . .' said Angus, desperately trying

to remember the name of Number Two's new wife, '... Priscilla?'

Number Two glanced over his shoulder, stepped out of the house and pulled the door closed behind him. He glared at Angus.

'Priscilla is very busy too,' he said. 'Unlike some mothers she chooses to stay at home and look after her children. You're too young to understand this, young man, but it's a lot of work, taking care of two young kids. Why doesn't your mother hire a nanny?'

It was Angus's turn to give Number Two a hard look.

'Mum doesn't hire nannies,' he said. 'Not since she hired Priscilla and you ran off with her.'

As Angus walked slowly home with Leo and Imogen, he saw that Leo was quietly crying.

'Don't worry,' he said, giving Leo a hug, 'I'll take you to the zoo some time. And tomorrow afternoon we'll go and see Imogen's dad.'

'Go away,' said Number Three.

Angus sighed. He'd half expected this. Mum was always saying male models were selfish and moody.

'Look,' said Number Three, running his fingers through his hair, 'me and your mother were together for two months. The kid was an accident.'

Angus put his hands over Imogen's ears. He wasn't exactly sure what Number Three meant, but he was sure Immie wouldn't like it.

'I made it clear to Marlene at the time,' said Number Three. 'I don't like kids.'

Angus glanced anxiously at Leo. From the way he was standing, Angus could see he was thinking about giving Number Three a very hard kick.

'What do you mean, an accident?' asked Angus, still keeping his hands over Imogen's ears.

Number Three ran a hand over his chin stubble. 'You know where babies come from, right?' he said.

Angus nodded.

'From mummies' tummies,' said Leo.

'Well, if mummies don't want more babies,' said Number Three, 'they can take pills to stop them having more. If they don't forget. Your mummy forgot. A lot.' He started to close the door.

'Wait,' said Angus. 'You're still Imogen's dad.'

'Sorry,' said Number Three, 'I'm really busy.'

From inside the flat Angus heard the sound of a cork coming out of a bottle and men giggling.

The door closed. Angus wasn't surprised. How could a man who couldn't even shave properly be a good father?

'Bumface,' shouted Imogen.

*

They went down the stairs and found Imogen's stroller and started to walk home.

'Well, that's it,' said Angus. 'We've run out of dads.'

'What about Number Four?' asked Leo.

'He's not a dad,' said Angus. 'He's a boyfriend.'

Leo's face fell. 'That means you can't be in the play,' he said.

Angus looked down at Leo's concerned expression. How could any dad not want to take this kid to the zoo immediately?

'Don't worry,' said Angus. 'I've got another plan.'

7

Angus stood outside the staffroom and rehearsed what he was going to say to Ms Lowry.

'Is it OK if I bring my five-year-old brother and my one-and-a-half-year-old sister to rehearsals?' he whispered to himself. 'As you know, my mum's an actor and she's keen for Leo and Imogen to start absorbing the magic of theatre.'

That sounded all right, and it wasn't a lie. Mum would be keen, if she knew.

Angus tapped on the staffroom door and reminded himself to explain to Ms Lowry that if Immie's nappy needed changing Ms Lowry wouldn't have to do it.

Mr Nash the assistant principal appeared at the door and glared at Angus.

'No teachers before school,' he growled. 'You know that.'

'I need to see Ms Lowry,' said Angus. 'It's really urgent.'

Ms Lowry's voice rang out from inside the staffroom. 'Is that Angus Solomon? I want to speak to him.'

Angus gave Mr Nash a relieved smile. Mr Nash grunted and went back inside.

Wonder what she wants to speak to me about, thought Angus. Hope it's to let me know the Tamagotchi's been found. Or that Russell Hinch has been transferred to a high-security prison school.

Ms Lowry appeared at the door. She didn't look like a woman who'd found a Tamagotchi.

Angus took a deep breath. 'Miss,' he began, 'is it OK . . .'

'Be quiet and listen,' said Ms Lowry. 'You, young man, have missed the last two rehearsals.'

Angus sagged. 'I can explain,' he said weakly, but when he met her eye he knew he couldn't. 'It'll never happen again, Miss,' he said, 'just as long as . . .'

'It's too late for promises,' said Ms Lowry. 'Plays only get produced when people are passionate and committed. I would have hoped you'd learnt that from your mother. But you're obviously neither passionate nor committed, Angus, and so you're out.'

Angus stared at her.

Out? What did she mean?

'Out of the play.'

His head felt as if she'd slapped it.

'I can't have unreliable people in speaking parts,' continued Ms Lowry. 'I'm sorry. You can help with the lighting.'

Angus wanted to scream at her to listen, to understand, to be fair, but before he could make a sound she told him to go and get ready for class and closed the door.

Angus had the petition circulating by lunch-time.

'What's this?' said Scott, peering at the page Angus had torn from his exercise book.

'It's for everyone to sign,' said Angus, 'so Ms Lowry'll see she's been unfair.'

Russell Hinch came over and took the page. 'I never sign anything without reading it first,' he said and started reading it out loud. 'We the undersigned reckon that Angus Solomon should not be chucked out of the school play just because he missed two rehearsals due to una-voidable private reasons and we reckon that if he promises not to miss any more he should be back in the school play and if he isn't we won't be in it either.'

'I'll cross that last bit out if you don't agree,' said Angus.

But he could tell from Russell's face that Russell didn't agree with any of it.

'I'm not signing this,' said Russell. 'No way.'

Angus wasn't surprised. Russell Hinch

wouldn't fight for justice if his baby sister was in gaol for bashing up sumo wrestlers.

Angus looked around at the other kids. 'What about the rest of you?' he said. 'Scott?'

He and Scott had been friends for ages. Scott would sign. And when Scott had, perhaps the others would.

Scott glanced at Russell, then stared at the ground. 'You dumped us,' he mumbled. 'We didn't dump you.'

'Dumped?' said Angus, shocked and hurt. 'What are you talking about? I haven't dumped anyone.'

'No?' sneered Russell. 'So where were you the last two afternoons?'

A thousand thoughts flew through Angus's head. Wild, crazy stories involving spies and submarines and newsagents. He knew they wouldn't work.

'Come on,' pleaded Angus. 'This isn't fair.'

'Yes it is,' said Renee Stokes. 'Doug Fawcett and Julie Cheng missed rehearsals and they're out of the play too.'

'At least you've got your girlfriend's shoulder to cry on,' smirked Russell, tearing up the petition.

Angus didn't cry until after Leo and Imogen were asleep.

It took him ages to settle them down.

'What about our Bumface story?' asked Leo indignantly.

'Not tonight,' said Angus, hoping the tears wouldn't start. Theirs or his. He read them a book instead, and finally they both fell asleep.

Angus went into his room, closed the door, threw himself onto his bed and wept.

After a long time, when there were no more tears, he listened anxiously, trying to hear if he'd woken Leo and Imogen. He'd tried to muffle the sound with his half-finished pirate costume, but Mum's old bolero jacket wasn't thick enough to absorb that much unhappiness.

He crept into Leo's room. Leo and Imogen were still asleep.

Then, because he was weak from crying, Angus had the thought he'd tried so hard not to have all the way home and all the way through dinner and all the way through wiping the walls and all the way through bathtime.

If it wasn't for you, he thought, looking at Leo and Imogen's sleeping faces, I'd still be in the play.

As soon as he had the thought he squashed it.

'I didn't mean it,' he whispered.

He kissed them both and pulled a frantically kicking stick insect from Leo's fist and flung it out the window with the thought.

He turned back to the sleeping kids.

They can't help having hopeless dads and a busy mum, he thought. None of us can.

He smoothed their sweaty hair off their foreheads and picked a bit of mashed potato and pumpkin off Imogen's scalp.

He couldn't imagine being without them.

He didn't want to be without them.

They'd only need him full-time for another sixteen or seventeen years and then the rest of his life would be his own.

Angus sighed.

It wasn't that long really.

All he had to desperately hope was that Mum didn't have any more babies.

Part Two

8

Angus tapped softly on Mum's bedroom door and pushed it open. In the faint morning light coming through the curtains, Angus could see she was still asleep.

He stepped forward to give her a gentle shake. He hated waking her, but it couldn't be helped. She was under contract and Angus was pretty sure that if she wasn't at the studio by eight she could be sued.

Suddenly he froze.

There was a man in the bed.

At first Angus didn't recognise him. Then he realised it was Number Four.

Gee, thought Angus, he looks different with his hair matted and dried dribble on his chin.

Another thought hit Angus and panic gripped him. Mum and Number Four were sleeping together. That could only mean one thing.

Sex.

Angus remembered what Number Three had said about Mum forgetting her pill.

He felt faint.

For a woman as busy as Mum, a woman who was always forgetting stuff, sex could easily mean another . . .

'Wheeeee!'

Imogen came tottering into the bedroom, shrieking happily. Before Angus could stop her, she clambered onto the bed and stuck her fingers up Number Four's nose.

'Urghhh,' groaned Number Four. His eyes squinted open. Then widened in horror as he saw what Imogen was doing.

Pouring his night-time glass of water down his tummy.

'Arghhh,' yelled Number Four as Imogen finished emptying the glass just before Angus grabbed it.

'Bathy Gavin,' chortled Imogen.

Mum opened her eyes and peered at her bedside clock.

'No,' she groaned. 'It's too early for all this. I need sleep.'

'Angus,' came Leo's excited yell from the hallway. 'Look.'

Leo staggered into the room carrying Geoffrey the mouse's cage. He plonked it on the bed. Bits of soggy lettuce and mouse droppings fell onto Number Four.

'Go away,' moaned Number Four.

'Look,' yelled Leo. 'Look what's happened to Geoffrey.'

Angus stared.

Geoffrey was lying exhausted on the floor of the cage. Nestling up to Geoffrey were some of the smallest mice Angus had ever seen.

'Geoffrey's got babies,' yelled Leo ecstatically.

Everyone stared.

'I don't believe it,' said Mum. 'Geoffrey's a girl.' She gave an exasperated sigh. 'Leo,' she said, 'that is the last time you get a pet from a kid at school.'

Leo started to protest loudly, snatching the cage back and banging into the bedside table, which made the bedside lamp topple onto Number Four's head.

Number Four yelled. Leo burst into tears. Imogen shrieked with excitement.

'Angus,' said Mum, grabbing Imogen. 'Help Gavin with the lamp and hand him a towel.'

Angus hardly heard her.

He was staring at the cage, mind racing.

If a mouse called Geoffrey couldn't help getting pregnant, a busy forgetful woman like Mum with a boyfriend she was in love with didn't stand a chance.

It was all right for Mum. If she got pregnant again, the TV writers would just write her big tummy into the script, like they had with

Imogen. The week after Immie was born, Mum had got a new TV baby called Craig.

Getting pregnant wasn't a problem for Mum. Or for Number Four, who could nick off any time he liked.

I'm the one, thought Angus miserably. I'm the one left holding the baby. I'm the one who'll never have a life.

'Angus,' yelled Mum.

While Angus handed Number Four a towel, he saw the way Number Four was scowling at Imogen and Leo and the baby mice.

Another bloke who didn't like kids or babies.

If Mum gets pregnant, thought Angus miserably, Number Four'll be out of here quicker than Number Three.

Angus had a horrible vision of the future. Of Number Five and Number Six and Number Forty Seven and Number Three Hundred And Sixty Two. And a never-ending stream of babies filling up Angus's whole life so that he'd still be changing nappies and wiping walls when he was ninety.

'Mum?' said Angus, trying to keep his voice steady.

'What?' said Mum, looking at him bleary-eyed.

'While I think of it,' said Angus. 'Have you taken your pill?'

9

Please Mum, begged Angus silently, please have your mobile switched on this time.

He picked up Dad's phone and rang her number again.

'This call,' said the familiar recorded voice, 'is to be diverted to another number.'

Angus left yet another message. 'Hi Mum, it's me again. Just in case you didn't get the other messages, don't forget to take your pill.'

He hung up and sighed. This was hard enough when Mum was at home. When she went away for a weekend it was a nightmare.

Angus looked anxiously at Dad's kitchen clock.

Ten past twelve. Mum should be at Number Four's beach house by now. She said she'd be there by lunchtime and she knows Leo and Imogen like their lunch early.

Imogen made a choking noise and Angus

went over and slapped her on the back. She coughed up a large lump of capsicum.

'That's not fair,' said Leo, glowering across the kitchen table. 'I didn't get a lump of capsicum that big.'

'Have this one,' said Angus, giving him Imogen's.

'Yuk,' said Leo.

Then an awful thought hit Angus. A thought so awful it made him feel like he had a giant lump of capsicum stuck in his chest.

What if Mum was already at the beach house, but the beach house was out of mobile range? What if she and Number Four were already doing sex? What if she hadn't seen the reminder note he'd stuck inside the lid of her suitcase or the one in her toilet bag or the one pinned to her nightie?

Angus raced back over to the phone.

Dad's girlfriend Kelly was there already. 'Excuse me, Angus,' she said, dialling. 'I need to make a call.'

Just my luck, thought Angus as he leapt across the kitchen and stopped Leo from poking his fork into a power socket. Trust Dad to have a girlfriend who's always on the phone.

Kelly finished her call and hung up. The phone rang immediately.

Angus prayed it was Mum calling to say she'd found his notes and heard all his messages and she'd taken her pill. Several in fact, just to be safe.

Kelly's voice changed and she started whispering dopey things into the phone. Obviously it was Dad.

Angus ground his teeth. Come on, he thought. Mum could be getting pregnant while you two are being romantic.

Kelly hung up. 'Your dad's been delayed at his creative writing class,' she said, 'so he's asked me to drop you at Leo's dad's. We'll have to leave right now.'

'Can I ring Mum first?' asked Angus desperately.

'Sorry,' said Kelly, 'no time. I've got an aerobics class in twenty minutes.'

Number Two was on the phone to his agent.

'No,' he was yelling. 'I won't. Impossible. Out of the question. No way.'

Priscilla tapped him on the arm. 'Dear,' she whispered. 'Angus and Leo and Imogen are here.'

He ignored her.

Angus sighed. Don't just tell him we're here, he thought, tell him I need to use the phone urgently.

'No,' yelled Number Two into the phone. 'I won't do it. I've got a major part in *Phantom of the Opera* and I will not play a pea in a frozen vegetable commercial. I want to be the carrot or nothing.'

Please, Angus silently begged the agent. Let him be the carrot so I can ring Mum.

'I won't,' yelled Number Two into the phone, his voice getting shrill. He threw his toast on the floor and stamped his foot. 'I won't, I won't, I won't!'

He hung up and kicked his toast across the kitchen. Leo picked it up and took a bite.

Number Two stared at him, startled, and then at Angus and Imogen.

'Ah . . .' he said, his voice going deep again. 'You're here. Good. There's been a change of plan. I've got to go to the theatre to do an interview and Priscilla's got to pick the boys up from clay modelling and take them to finger painting, so I'll have to drop you three off.'

'Can I ring Mum first,' asked Angus desperately.

'No time,' said Number Two. 'Do it at Imogen's dad's.'

'What are you lot doing here?' said Number Three.

Angus had feared this. According to Mum, Number Three had agreed to have them for part of the weekend, but she'd obviously forgotten what short memories male models had.

Angus peered out the stairwell window. Number Two's car was already out of sight.

He turned back to Number Three, thinking fast. 'We're doing a play at school,' he said, 'and Ms Lowry needs help with the makeup and wigs and seeing as you're one of the country's top male models I thought I'd ask you.'

Number Three frowned at Angus. 'I might be able to spare some time,' he said. His face softened a bit behind his stubble. 'Come in and tell me more about it.'

Inside the flat a bloke was on the phone. Another one was sprawled in a beanbag talking on a mobile.

'This play,' said Number Three. 'Will there be a printed programme?'

Angus felt like he had several kilos of capsicum trying to burst out of his chest. Mum and Number Four would almost certainly be naked and in bed by now.

'There'll be a programme,' said Angus frantically, 'but it might just be photocopied.' He was about to ask Number Three how urgent the two blokes' calls were when he realised that Imogen had toddled out onto the balcony.

It had a metal fence round it with big gaps.

It was two floors up.

Angus flung himself towards her, but Number Three got there first and scooped her up.

'Jeez,' panted Number Three, 'that was close.'

Angus couldn't say anything till the capsicum went back down his throat.

Imogen chuckled and stroked Number Three's stubble. Number Three squinted at her. 'Look at that,' he said. 'She's got my eyes.'

Behind them in the flat, the bloke on the phone hung up and started dialling again.

'Jeez,' said Number Three. 'Is that the time? I've got a footy match at two-thirty.'

Dad opened his front door and stared at them, puzzled.

Angus didn't even say g'day, just pushed past and ran into the kitchen and snatched up the phone and dialled.

Mum answered.

'Angus,' she said. 'What's wrong?'

Angus nearly fainted with relief. Then he nearly fainted with concern. Mum's voice sounded low and purry. Like people's in movies did when they'd just had sex or ice-cream.

Please, begged Angus silently, let it be ice-cream.

'Mum,' he said, 'have you taken your pill?'

Angus heard Mum give a long, low sigh. He realised her voice wasn't sexy, it was angry.

'Darling,' she said. 'Angus. Please. Can I just have one weekend to myself? That's not a lot to ask, is it?'

'No,' said Angus. 'Have you taken it?'

'Oh, for Pete's sake,' yelled Mum.

Angus heard a rustling and a crackling and

liquid pouring into a glass and Mum swallowing.

'There,' said Mum. 'I've taken it. Are you happy now?'

Angus murmured that he was.

'Please, darling,' said Mum, 'have a nice weekend with the dads and I'll see you all tomorrow afternoon and only ring me if there's an emergency, OK?'

You mean another emergency, thought Angus.

He said goodbye and hung up and flopped into a kitchen chair. 'I can't take much more of this,' he croaked.

He thought of having to do it every weekend. And every weekday. He thought of trying to ring Mum from the school staffroom without Mr Nash catching him.

'There's got to be a better way,' said Angus to the salt and pepper shakers.

Dad came in looking perplexed. 'Bit of a misunderstanding,' he said. 'I've got a meeting with a book illustrator in town at three. I'll have to drop you back at Leo's dad's.'

Priscilla sat Angus and Leo and Imogen on a settee with a towel over it.

'Robert's still at the theatre,' she said, 'but he should be home soon.'

Angus smiled at the two elderly people who were sitting holding cups of tea and looking at him.

'Angus,' said Priscilla. 'This is my parents, Mr and Mrs Bridges.'

'Hello,' said Mr and Mrs Bridges.

'Hello,' said Angus. 'This is Leo, your grandson-in-law, and Imogen, your step-granddaughter-in-law once removed.'

He hoped that was right.

Mr and Mrs Bridges smiled awkwardly.

Mrs Bridges took off her watch and swung it in front of Imogen's face.

'This is my very old watch,' said Mrs Bridges.

Imogen ignored her.

'If you listen carefully,' said Mrs Bridges to Leo, 'it goes tick tick tick.'

'That's because it's a watch,' said Leo.

'Clever boy,' said Mrs Bridges, smiling. She turned to Angus. 'You're a thoughtful-looking young man,' she said. 'Is there anything you'd like to know about my watch?'

'Not really,' said Angus. 'But I would like to know if there's anything a woman with a hopeless memory can use so she doesn't get pregnant during sex.'

Mr Bridges seemed to be having trouble breathing. Mrs Bridges put her watch back on and looked at the floor. There was a long silence.

'Do you like the fruitcake, Mum?' asked Priscilla.

Angus sighed.

10

The chemist shop was packed.

Angus didn't think he could go through with it.

Run, he told himself. Just turn and run.

But he didn't. He took a deep breath instead.

Rather than take the stroller into the shop and bump into people, Angus made Leo and Imogen wait near the entrance.

A mum had the same idea. 'Stay here and don't touch anything on these shelves,' she said to her three little kids. 'Or I'll smack you.'

'Same goes for you,' said Angus to Leo and Imogen.

Leo looked at Angus, his bottom lip quivering. 'You wouldn't smack us,' he said, 'would you?'

Angus gave him a hug. Kids without proper dads could be real sooks.

'No,' he said, 'I wouldn't smack you.'

'Cause if you did,' said Leo, 'we'd smack you back.'

Angus moved into the shop, examining the shelves, hoping to find what he was after. If only he knew what the thing was called or what it looked like.

Ms Lowry had been no help at all. Angus had asked her at lunchtime. 'Excuse me Miss, what would stop a forgetful mother getting pregnant during sex?'

But Ms Lowry had been distracted by Russell Hinch trying to flush another kid's bag down the dunny. 'Don't bother me now,' she'd said. 'We'll be doing more human reproduction once the school play's over.'

The Internet in the library had been no help at all when he'd typed in 'human reproduction/ forgetful mothers'.

Angus went along another shelf, picked up a jar and studied the label.

It was bath salts.

I'm groping in the dark here, thought Angus. Perhaps I'd better ask.

All day he'd been trying to decide whether to risk asking the chemist, who was almost as old as Mr Bridges and might have a breathing problem too. Plus it was a pretty embarrassing thing to ask for in public, specially if it turned out the thing didn't exist, or you were in the wrong shop and you should be in the hardware store.

'You there,' said a stern voice. 'Stay right where you are.'

Angus spun round.

The chemist, red-faced, was hurrying towards him. 'I'm sick of you kids coming in here shoplifting,' said the chemist. 'Empty out that school bag.'

Angus stared at him, insides sinking. Not again. People were staring and whispering.

'Do I have to?' said Angus miserably.

'Yes,' said the chemist. 'If you haven't been stealing you've got nothing to worry about, have you?'

That's what you think, thought Angus.

He unzipped his bag and tipped everything onto the shop floor. Books. Lunchbox. Gym shoes.

Dirty nappy.

The chemist stared. The customers stared. Angus felt his face burning.

'I'm looking after it for someone else,' he said.

The chemist snorted. 'Yes, well next time don't bring it in here.'

While Angus packed his things away, the chemist put the nappy into a plastic bag and gave it to one of his shop assistants. Then he turned back to Angus.

'So,' he said. 'What can I help you with?'

'Um,' whispered Angus. 'Something for my mother.'

'Ah,' said the chemist. 'A Mother's Day present. These bath salts are always popular. Or this moisturiser. Stop her getting rough skin on her hands when she does the washing up.'

Angus took a deep breath and explained that it wasn't actually her getting rough skin on her hands he was worried about.

On the train, Angus hoped he hadn't made a mistake buying Leo and Imogen ice-creams. There was a green trickle running down Leo's wrist and green droplets hanging off his chin. Imogen was worse. She had so much ice-cream on her face she looked like a Martian.

Oh well, thought Angus, they're happy.

He looked at the address on the back of the leaflet the chemist had given him, then checked the map on the wall above their seat.

Two more stops.

Angus studied the front of the leaflet. Family Planning Clinic, it said, and the word contraception was used quite a lot. Angus hoped contraception was another word for not getting pregnant. Possibly even another word for people with hopeless memories not getting pregnant.

I hope that chemist understood what I'm after, thought Angus. I've wasted a heap of time and money if a Family Planning Clinic turns out to be a place for families who want to plan where to put their furniture.

Then he saw the words Birth Control on the leaflet.

That sounds like what I'm looking for, he thought.

He realised Leo was nudging him.

'Look at them,' said Leo, pointing across the carriage.

'Don't point,' whispered Angus.

He looked at the family Leo was pointing at. A mum and dad were gazing fondly at their two kids. All four of them were eating icy poles and not one of them had a single drip on any part of their body.

A pang of jealousy stabbed through Angus.

'Are they a TV family?' asked Leo.

'No,' said Angus. 'Shhhh.' But he was tempted to lean across and ask the family where you could get non-drip ice-creams and marriages that lasted.

Leo gave a yelp and burst into tears. Angus saw that Leo's ice-cream had broken into two and fallen on the floor.

It was quickly becoming a puddle. Leo bawled even harder.

'If you'd eaten it more quickly,' said Angus, 'that wouldn't have happened.'

The parents across the carriage glanced over and Angus could see they agreed with him.

Leo gave him a hurt and angry look.

Angus sighed. Poor kid. He wished he didn't

have to be so strict. He wished he could do what any decent big brother would do. Give Leo a hug and buy him another ice-cream when they got off the train.

Sometimes it was a real pain being a parent.

The Family Planning Clinic was a big brick building with all its blinds down so Angus couldn't see if it was full of furniture diagrams or not.

He steered the stroller into a bus shelter a little way down the street and put the brake on.

'I won't be long,' he said to Leo and Imogen. 'Stay here and count buses.'

'I want to count ants,' said Leo.

'Buses and ants,' said Angus.

He saw that Imogen was looking dangerously damp.

'When I'm back in a couple of minutes I'll buy you another nappy,' he said to her.

'Gussy nappy,' said Imogen.

'And another ice-cream for me,' said Leo, looking at him fiercely. 'Or I won't stay.'

Angus sighed and nodded. That's OK, he thought. That's blackmail and parents are allowed to give in to that.

He crept into the building.

The waiting room was empty except for a receptionist behind a desk. After a bit, as Angus watched from behind a big pot-plant in the foyer, she got up and went out through a door marked Staff Only.

Angus ducked into the waiting room, his heart pounding.

It looked like the right place. There were human reproduction diagrams on the wall, just like Ms Lowry's only neater.

Angus peered around for leaflets, brochures, pamphlets, catalogues, anything with the words Birth Control or Forgetful Mothers on it.

He saw a rack of leaflets and was heading towards it when he heard the door click behind him.

He whirled round.

A girl about his age had just come in. She had dark hair and dark eyes and was wearing a school uniform he didn't recognise.

She winked at him.

Angus felt his face go hot. He looked at his watch. 'Parents,' he muttered and went and sat down in the far corner of the room and pretended to read a magazine.

The magazine was about rock-climbing. It had nothing in it about how to stop forgetful rock-climbers getting pregnant.

Pathetic, thought Angus. What about all the rock-climbers who've got hopeless memories because they've banged their heads on rocks?

He got out his pen and pretended to do the rock-climbing crossword while he watched the girl rummaging through the leaflets.

She finished rummaging and went out.

Angus waited two seconds and then leapt across the room towards the rack and was just about to start grabbing leaflets when the receptionist came back in.

'Yes?' she said. 'Can I help you?'

'Um . . .' said Angus. 'No, I'm . . . er . . . fine thanks.'

The receptionist stared at him. Angus wondered if she was going to make him empty out his bag.

'I've come for some information,' he said.

'No you haven't,' said the receptionist, looking hard at the pen in his hand. 'You've come because all your mates told you how much fun they had sneaking in here and writing smutty comments on our walls and publications.'

'No,' protested Angus. 'Honest . . .'

'Get out,' said the receptionist, 'and if you come back I'll ring the police.'

Angus opened his mouth to plead. She picked up the phone. He closed his mouth and went out.

He hurried along the street, chest hurting with stress and disappointment. He tried not to think of all the babies Mum would soon be having.

Oh well, he thought miserably. Life can't get any worse than this.

He got to the bus shelter and it did.

The bus shelter was empty.

Leo and Imogen were gone.

11

Angus felt sick with panic.

He peered frantically up and down the street, across the road, under the bench.

No Leo and Imogen.

Please, thought Angus desperately, a sob forcing its way out of his throat, please don't let them have got on a bus. He had an awful vision of Leo and Imogen being arrested for not having a ticket, or worse, huddled together at a deserted bus depot, abandoned, lost, terrified.

Angus sprinted back towards the clinic to ask the receptionist to call the police.

Then he heard a scream.

'Imogen?' he yelled. He looked around wildly. The scream had come from behind some bushes. He flung himself at them.

The bushes were a sort of hedge. Angus tore his way through, not caring that twigs scraped him and branches slapped him around the head.

He staggered out the other side and found himself in a children's playground and there, at his feet, gazing up at him with big adoring eyes, was a dog.

'Imogen,' yelled Angus frantically. 'Leo.'

The dog ran off.

'Bumface,' shrieked a happy voice.

Angus turned. In the middle of the playground, sitting next to her stroller at the base of an adventure gym, was Imogen.

Angus ran to her. 'Where's Leo?' he yelled.

'Here,' shouted Leo, swinging towards them on the end of a rope and sprawling into the dust next to Imogen.

Imogen screamed with laughter.

Angus wanted to roar at them that they were naughty, disobedient children, but suddenly he felt so wobbly with relief he could only sit down next to them. 'I told you to stay in the bus shelter,' he said.

'There was a worm,' said Leo sadly, 'and it was lonely in the bus shelter. It cuddled up to me. I had to find it some other worms.'

Angus sighed. With most kids you'd think they were making that up, but with Leo you knew it was true.

Leo's face brightened. 'Then we got lost and a pirate rescued us.'

'Pirate?' said Angus, frowning. 'What pirate?'

'Look out!' roared a voice.

Angus turned to see a yelling figure swinging towards him on the end of the rope, hair flying. The sun was in Angus's eyes, and for a second he had a crazy thought.

Bumface?

The figure crashed into Angus, knocking the frown off his face and sending him head over heels in the dust.

After a bit, when he'd checked none of his bones were broken, Angus opened his eyes.

A face was very close to his. A grinning, dark-eyed, dust-streaked face. It was the girl from the clinic.

'G'day,' she said. 'Sorry.'

'This is Rindi the pirate,' said Leo. 'She's not just a story pirate, she's real. She's teaching me pirate rope swings.'

'Rindi,' gurgled Imogen, hugging Rindi's leg.

Angus sat up and brushed himself off and gave Rindi a sour glance. Who did she think she was, knocking him over and getting friendly with his family?

Then he remembered how panicked he'd been when he thought Leo and Imogen had gone.

'Thanks for looking after them,' he muttered.

'Leo told me you're into pirates,' said Rindi. 'He explained you don't get much time to play them with him cause you're so busy.'

'That's right,' said Angus warily. He wondered what the youngest age was that journalists could start their careers and whether they were allowed to disguise themselves as schoolgirls.

'Hope you don't mind me elbowing in,' said Rindi. 'I've had a great time.'

'No,' said Angus. 'Well, um, we should be going now. My mum'll be finished at the clinic any minute.'

'No she won't,' said Leo. 'She's at the studio.'

Angus thought about strangling Leo. It was hard to get a good grip, though, when your hands were clammy with embarrassment.

Rindi was grinning at him again. Her face was so friendly that Angus was tempted to grin back, but he didn't, just in case.

To give himself something else to do, he checked Imogen's nappy. Except it wasn't her nappy, it was some sort of white cloth wrapped round her.

'Imogen's nappy burst when she came off the slide,' said Rindi, 'so I put my sports T-shirt on her instead.'

Angus stared at Rindi in surprise. 'Thanks,' he said. That didn't seem like something a journalist would do. Hand over a T-shirt for a toddler to poo on. Mum reckoned journalists didn't even like it if you spilt wine on their slacks.

'Want a go on the pirate rope?' asked Rindi.

Angus didn't know what to say.

'It's great,' yelled Leo. 'Have a go.'

Rindi put the rope into Angus's hand. 'You're not chicken, are you?' she grinned.

'No,' said Angus indignantly. 'I do this heaps.'

As he climbed up to the platform he wished he'd told Rindi the truth. That he only did it heaps in his imagination. That he hadn't done it in real life for five and a half years. Not since Leo was born.

Angus stood on the edge of the platform, shaking with fear.

Pull yourself together, he told himself. If you've got the guts to yell at Russell Hinch, you've got the guts to swing on this dumb rope.

Angus gripped the rope tighter, closed his eyes and jumped.

As he swung through the air, scalp tingling in the breeze, he heard himself yelling.

It wasn't a yell of fear.

It was a joyful pirate yell.

He let go of the rope and sprawled in the dust near Rindi and the others.

'Good one,' yelled Leo.

'Gussy Bumface,' shrieked Imogen.

'Bumface is a great name for a pirate,' laughed Rindi.

As he blinked the dust out of his eyes, Angus found he was hardly embarrassed at all. 'Imogen came up with it,' he said.

'Hey,' shouted Leo excitedly. 'Let's go to Bumface's secret island.'

'All right,' said Rindi.

'All right,' said Angus.

They played for ages.

Angus kept an anxious eye on his watch, but each time he decided they had to go, Rindi and the little kids persuaded him to do one more pirate raid.

He didn't need much persuading.

As he swung happily on the rope, he remembered that this was what life used to be like, a long time ago. For a fleeting second he wondered what had gone wrong.

Then, as he hit the ground, he remembered.

His insides sank.

'What's up?' said Rindi. 'Pirate injury?'

Angus shook his head. 'It's OK,' he said.

'Leo told me about your mum,' said Rindi gently. 'I reckon she's cool. I've seen her on telly heaps. But I can understand why you don't want her to have any more kids. My cousin in India has to look after eight little brothers and sisters and he got his first grey hair when he was only fifteen.'

Angus stared at her in shock. She knew about Mum. But something in her concerned expression made him start to relax.

'Bad luck about the school play,' said Rindi. 'Leo told me about that as well.'

'Leo,' yelled Angus, exasperated. 'Is there anything you didn't tell her?'

'I didn't tell her about Geoffrey,' said Leo. He turned to Rindi. 'Geoffrey had babies.'

Angus tried to stay cross, but Rindi was grinning so widely that Angus couldn't stop himself grinning too.

Then he remembered something and was suddenly serious again.

'Rindi,' he said urgently. 'About my mum. It's a secret. A total secret. Do you understand?'

Rindi was staring at the ground. 'Don't worry,' she said quietly. 'I'm good at secrets.'

Angus prayed she was. He looked at her serious expression and suddenly he felt that she was the first person in a long time he could trust.

This is dopey, he thought happily. I've known her about two hours.

Rindi's face brightened.

'Did you get the information you wanted from the clinic?' she asked.

Angus's insides sank. With everything that had happened, he'd forgotten what a disaster the clinic had been.

'Don't worry,' said Rindi. 'I got heaps.'

The train home was really full. Angus had hoped that Leo and Imogen's new ice-creams would keep the crowds back a bit, but no luck. People were pressing into them from all sides.

While Leo and Imogen slurped and dripped, he and Rindi studied the leaflets she'd got from the clinic.

'There's heaps of good stuff here,' said Rindi excitedly. 'If you used all this stuff you wouldn't get pregnant in a million years.'

Angus glanced anxiously at the other passengers. He was relieved to see they were all looking out the window or at the ceiling or at the floor. The last thing he needed was some nosy passenger thinking the leaflets were stolen and kicking up a fuss.

'What I'm looking for,' said Rindi, thumbing through the leaflets, 'is something cheap and foolproof where you don't have to rely on chemicals or blokes.'

Angus thought about Dad and Numbers Two to Four and nodded understandingly. He was about to ask Rindi how many brothers and sisters she had and whether her mum was forgetful too, when Leo gave a howl. His ice-cream was on the floor in two pieces.

'You poor thing,' said Rindi. 'I reckon they don't make ice-creams strong enough for little kids.' She dug into her school bag and pulled out a pencil case. 'Here,' she said, handing Leo some coloured pencils and a leaflet. 'Would you like to colour in a condom?'

Leo's eyes shone and he set to work.

Angus went back to reading and soon his eyes were shining too. There it was, on the leaflet in his hand, exactly the thing he'd been hoping to find. He showed Rindi.

'It's called an intra-uterine device,' he said. 'It's a little plastic and metal thing and once it's fitted inside a woman she can forget about it for ages, which my mum would almost certainly do, and she still won't get pregnant.'

Rindi studied the leaflet. Angus glanced at the other passengers. They were still minding their own business.

'Hmmm,' said Rindi, studying the drawing of the intra-uterine device. 'Not bad, but I like the look of this better.' She pointed to a drawing on her leaflet.

Angus looked. It was called a diaphragm. He didn't have a clue how to say it.

'There's a pronunciation guide,' said Rindi. 'Die-a-fram.'

'Die-a-fram,' said Leo.

'Gussy-fram,' yelled Imogen.

'It goes inside too,' said Rindi, 'but it's bendy rubber so it can be taken out and washed and used over and over.'

'But,' said Angus, studying the leaflet, 'don't mothers have to remember to put it in each time before they do sex?'

Rindi nodded. Angus looked at her, concerned.

'Are you sure your mum's got that good a memory?' he said.

Rindi looked at him for a long time. Finally she spoke.

'It's not for my mum,' she said. 'It's for me.'

Angus stared. After a while he realised he wasn't the only one. The people standing around them had completely lost interest in the window and the ceiling and the floor and were all gaping at Rindi.

'I won't be using it yet,' said Rindi. 'I just want to be prepared for the future.'

Angus digested this. Boy, he thought, I wish Mum was that good at planning ahead.

He gave the people staring a stare back. They all looked away. If I was braver, thought Angus, I'd tell them to give her a round of applause.

Leo finished colouring the condom at almost the same moment Imogen finished eating her ice-cream. Rindi spent the time until her station telling them both how clever they were.

Her stop was two before Angus's.

When it was time to say goodbye, Angus touched her on the arm.

'Thanks,' he said.

He felt himself blushing.

Rindi grinned. 'Any time, Bumface,' she said.

'If you do ever have kids,' said Angus, 'you'll make a really great parent.'

At first, Angus didn't understand why Rindi's face was clouding over. It was only after she'd muttered 'Yeah, that's what everyone reckons', and picked up her school bag and started to move away that he realised he must have said something wrong.

'Wait,' he said. 'I'm sorry. I didn't mean to . . .'

She jumped off the train and started to run.

'Rindi,' yelled Angus. 'What's wrong?'

He moved towards the door, but the train was already pulling out of the station.

He caught a last glimpse of Rindi's face, tense and unhappy.

'What's wrong?' said Angus again, to himself this time.

'She's upset,' said Leo.

Angus sighed, puzzled and concerned.

Sometimes it wasn't only little kids who didn't understand.

12

Angus tipped Leo and Imogen's breakfast cereal into their bowls. Something small and plastic tumbled out of the box.

'Me,' screamed Imogen.

'I want it,' yelled Leo.

'It's for Mummy,' said Angus, putting the plastic soldier on the shelf next to her Logie.

In his head he wrote a letter to the cereal manufacturers.

'Dear Sir/Madam,

Have you ever thought of putting contraceptives in cereal boxes? I reckon contraceptives would be even more popular than plastic soldiers. I'd buy any brand of cereal with an intra-uterine device in it.' —

Angus yawned.

He'd been awake half the night trying to think where he could get one. That and worrying about Rindi.

Chemists didn't sell them, he knew that. If he went back to the Family Planning Clinic he'd be arrested and he was pretty sure the police wouldn't have any.

Angus opened the fridge door to get the milk and a light went on in his head at exactly the same moment as in the fridge.

A factory. There must be an intra-uterine device factory somewhere. With delivery trucks. Russell Hinch's uncle was a truck driver and Russell reckoned his uncle's place was full of stuff that had fallen off the back of trucks.

It would be a huge risk, asking Russell Hinch if his uncle knew any intra-uterine device truck drivers. Russell could easily go ballistic and tell the whole school.

It's a risk I've got to take, thought Angus as he gave Leo and Imogen their cereal and Imogen tipped hers into her orange juice.

Angus went to the laundry to check Rindi's T-shirt. It had been soaking in stain-remover all night, but when he lifted it out of the bucket he saw it still needed another day or so.

No rush, he thought sadly. I'll probably never see her again.

Angus started folding some washing and Mum came in, bleary-eyed, pulling her dressing gown on.

'Hello darling,' she yawned. 'I didn't wake

you when I got in last night cause it was a bit late. Here, I got you all a prezzie.'

Angus knew what it would be even before Mum handed them over. Sesame bars from the studio canteen. Whenever Mum rang to say she was going to be late, she always brought home sesame bars.

Pity the canteen doesn't sell birth control stuff, thought Angus wearily.

Mum rubbed her eyes and yawned again. Angus saw she was looking pretty weary herself. Either that or depressed. If she was depressed, Angus hoped it was because Number Four had gone off her sexually.

Number Four came into the laundry wrapped in a sheet. He rubbed his eyes and put his arms round Mum.

Angus sighed. It didn't look as though he had.

'G'day, Angus,' said Number Four. 'How you going?'

'OK,' said Angus. He didn't mention that he was almost throwing up from Number Four's stale cigarette smell.

Mum didn't seem to mind. She gave Number Four a big wet kiss.

She must really love him, thought Angus gloomily. He had a horrible vision of Mum and Number Four getting married on the show her network did where people had weddings live on air, ending with Mum turning to the camera with confetti in her hair and announcing she was pregnant.

Not if I can help it, thought Angus.

'I'm going for a shower,' said Mum.

Angus went back to folding the washing. He felt Number Four's hand on his shoulder.

'Mother's Day's coming up,' said Number Four, keeping his voice low. 'I reckon it'd be really good if you got something for your mum.'

Angus gave Number Four a long look.

'I'm getting her something,' he said. 'It's under control.'

'This stroller's out of control,' said Leo as he struggled to help Angus push it. 'When Immie started crying and you tried to go faster, you bent the wheel on the kerb. It's out of control.'

'No it's not,' said Angus wearily, 'it's just hard to push. Out of control means you can't stop something.'

'Like you can't stop Immie crying cause she's teething?' said Leo.

Angus nodded wearily.

'Like you can't stop my finger hurting after that snail bit me just now?' said Leo.

Angus nodded wearily.

'Like you can't stop Mrs Bennett getting suspicious about Mum?' said Leo.

Angus nodded wearily. 'Leo,' he said, 'that's enough.'

'Like you can't stop Russell Hinch telling the whole school you're doing sex with your girl-friend?' said Leo. 'Just cause you asked him about intra-submarine devices?'

'Leo,' yelled Angus, 'that's enough.'

Leo's eyes filled with tears, just like they did when his dad yelled at him.

Angus gave Leo a hug. 'Sorry,' he said. 'It's me I'm angry with, for being an idiot.'

'You're not an idiot,' said Leo. 'You're just too busy.'

'I'm an idiot,' said Angus bitterly. 'I'm an idiot for talking about contraceptives with Russell Hinch. He didn't know what they were till I told him.'

Angus shuddered at the memory of how Russell's face had lit up and how he'd raced off yelling to his mates that Angus Solomon was doing it.

Angus realised Imogen had started crying again. He took a tube of numbing gel out of his pocket and gently rubbed some on her gums.

'I a idiot,' said Imogen tearfully.

'No you're not,' said Leo. 'Angus is.'

Soon Imogen stopped crying.

It's good stuff, this numbing gel, thought Angus. They should make one for people to rub on their chests after school to numb the pain of seeing all the other kids going off to rehearsals.

'This intra-submarine device,' said Leo. 'Where are you going to get one?'

'Don't know,' said Angus. 'I'm still thinking.'

'The navy might have them,' said Leo.

They'd just pushed the stroller round the next corner when a person dropped out of a tree.

The person landed behind them with a pirate yell. For a second Angus thought it was Russell Hinch. Sprung, he told himself miserably, after I was so careful not to mention anything about Mum.

But it wasn't Russell Hinch, it was Rindi.

'Hello,' she said, grinning and shaking leaves out of her hair.

Angus stared at her, flabbergasted. 'How did you ... ?'

'Leo told me yesterday how you always go to the childcare centre after school,' said Rindi.

'I told her about the fish,' said Leo. 'How they like crayons.'

Angus watched as Rindi gave Leo a hug, her dark eyes flashing with amusement.

'Rindi,' yelled Imogen excitedly, 'Rindi.'

Rindi gave her a hug too.

As the shock of Rindi's entrance wore off, Angus realised how glad he was to see her.

She turned to him. 'Sorry I was so moody yesterday,' she said. 'I get like that sometimes.'

'So does Angus,' said Leo.

'I was worried about you,' said Angus.

Rindi gave him a warm smile. 'Thanks,' she said. 'But I didn't bust a gut to get all the way over here just to talk about my dumb old moods. I've got some news.'

She rummaged in her school bag. After a bit she swore and tipped everything out onto the footpath. Angus stared. There were clothes and books all mixed up with half-eaten food and lolly wrappers. It was worse than Leo's bag.

'Look,' said Leo. 'She's got peanut butter in her shoe like me. You said only babies do that.'

Angus gave him a glare. Mostly so none of them would see he was feeling a bit left out.

Rindi handed Angus a crumpled sheet of paper with what looked like barbecue sauce on it. It was a photocopy of a page from the street directory. A street corner in the city was circled in green texta.

'I've been ringing up medical equipment suppliers,' said Rindi. 'On Friday in the city there's a medical convention. There'll be heaps of medical equipment on display, including samples of contraceptives.'

Angus felt a big grin creep across his face.

'Free samples?' he said.

'Not exactly free,' said Rindi.

'For sale?' he asked.

Rindi shook her head.

Angus felt his grin disappearing. 'So how do we get them?' he asked.

'Think of it as a pirate raid,' said Rindi.

Angus started to feel a bit sick. 'There might be security guards,' he said, 'and people with dentists drills.'

'Would Bumface let that stop him?' said Rindi quietly.

'No,' said Angus. 'Not in a play.'

'If your mum gets pregnant,' said Rindi, 'it won't be in a play, will it? It'll be in real life.'

Angus looked at her for a long time, his brain racing.

She was right, but he still felt sick.

13

Angus strolled around the playground trying to look innocent and not in any way like a person who was planning to raid a medical convention after school.

It seemed to be working. The other kids were ignoring him.

Lucky I'm a good actor, thought Angus.

Then Scott came sprinting up to Russell Hinch breathless and wide-eyed. 'The police are coming to the school,' he gasped.

Angus felt his blood chill. How could the police have found out? Rindi wouldn't have blabbed, he was sure. He'd only known her a couple of days, but he could tell she was the sort of person who wouldn't blab, not even if the police were torturing her by making her tidy her school bag.

It must have been Leo. He must have told another kid in infants and a teacher must have heard.

'When?' Angus asked Scott. 'When are they getting here?'

'Monday,' said Scott. 'They're coming to talk to us about modern crime prevention techniques. I heard Mr Nash telling Ms Lowry.'

Angus leant against the tuck shop wall, weak with relief. I'm too jumpy, he said to himself. Bumface wouldn't over-react like that.

While he breathed deeply, Angus remembered he hadn't been the only one. Russell Hinch had gone into a panic too. He'd looked as alarmed as Angus had felt, and his hand had shot guiltily to his school bag.

Stacy's Tamagotchi, thought Angus as he watched Russell bash Scott round the head with the bag. I bet he's got a secret pocket in there somewhere.

Angus was trying to think what to do about it when he saw something that made Stacy's Tamagotchi suddenly seem not quite so important.

Number Two, coming out of the school office with Ms Lowry. The teacher looked around, saw Angus and waved him over.

Angus thought hard as he crossed the playground. Could Leo have blabbed about the medical convention to Number Two? Didn't seem likely. Leo hadn't seen his dad this week. Perhaps Number Two had suffered a guilt attack and rung Leo while Angus was in the garden hosing down the stroller.

'Hello, Angus,' said Number Two.

'Hello,' said Angus nervously.

Number Two wasn't smiling. But then he hardly ever smiled in real life. Ms Lowry was smiling.

'Your stepfather has very kindly offered to help me stage the battle scene in the school play,' she beamed.

Of course. Angus was so relieved he didn't bother explaining that Number Two was actually his ex-stepfather.

Some Year Four kids had gathered and were staring at Number Two's *Phantom of the Opera* T-shirt. 'Ah,' said Number Two. 'Young auto-graph hunters.' He got out his pen.

The Year Four kids ran away.

Number Two's mouth fell open briefly. Then he muttered something about being late for an interview, said a theatrical goodbye to Ms Lowry, a quick one to Angus, and left.

Ms Lowry turned to Angus. 'This is so exciting,' she said, 'having both your stepfathers bringing their professional expertise to the play.'

Angus stared. Both stepfathers? Number Three must have accepted his invitation too.

'We've had a brilliant idea,' Ms Lowry said. 'We're going to get the audience to dress up as pirates too. Brilliant, eh?'

Angus nodded. Why is she telling me this? he wondered.

'I've decided,' Ms Lowry continued, 'that in

recognition of your family's contribution, I'm going to let you back into the play.'

Angus was speechless with delight.

Then he remembered something. He opened his mouth to explain about bringing Leo and Imogen to rehearsals. Before he could start, Ms Lowry held up her hand.

'I'm letting you back in on one condition,' she said. 'You must be at today's rehearsal after school. You can make a phonecall from the office if you need to.'

Angus felt his insides plummet. 'Not today,' he pleaded.

Ms Lowry sighed. 'Angus,' she said, 'you have to learn that part of growing up is doing things you don't really want to do.'

'I've got to be somewhere after school,' said Angus.

'Where?' said Ms Lowry.

'I can't say,' said Angus miserably.

Ms Lowry's jaw went taut. 'If you want to be in the play,' she said, 'be at rehearsal after school today. It's your choice.'

She turned and went into the office. Angus walked slowly away, wishing desperately he could have told her the truth.

Then she'd have understood.

School plays are important, she'd have agreed, but sometimes it's more important to be a pirate in real life.

*

The convention hall was big and brightly lit, with rows of display stands full of medical equipment and groups of eager salespeople wearing coloured blazers.

There were also, standing next to the coffee machine, two security guards.

Rindi stiffened when Angus pointed them out. But only for a moment. 'I don't think they've seen us,' she said. 'Come on, let's find the birth control stuff.'

Together they pushed the stroller along the rows of stands. It took ages, partly because of the bent wheel and partly because Leo kept asking questions.

'What's that?' he said for the millionth time, pointing to what looked to Angus like an inflatable toilet seat.

'Come on,' said Angus.

'Come on,' said Imogen.

'Don't pull,' said Leo. 'I think it's an intra-submarine device.'

Angus tried to steer Leo away, but it was too late. A salesman at the stand had seen them and was smiling and coming over.

'G'day, kids,' he boomed. 'Having a look round while dad's working, eh? Who's dad with?' The salesman waved his arm up and down the aisle.

Angus saw Leo open his mouth to say *Phantom of the Opera* or 'Priscilla'. Before

Angus could get his hand over Leo's mouth, Rindi said, 'Axis Computer Systems.'

'Ah,' said the salesman vaguely. 'I haven't caught their stand yet.' He went over to greet a customer.

'Brilliant performance,' Angus whispered to Rindi. 'You should be in my school play.'

'It's true,' said Rindi indignantly. 'My dad's their sales manager. The bloke didn't ask if he was here, did he?'

'Well, it was quick thinking, anyway,' said Angus.

They pushed the wobbly stroller down the aisle, trying their best to look like bored kids while giving each stand a long stare.

Suddenly Rindi nudged Angus.

'There,' she said, 'to our left. Contraceptives.'

Angus pretended to be checking Imogen's nappy, which was pretty full. He peered at the stand through the handles of the stroller.

Diaphragms.

Intra-uterine devices.

All stuck on little boards under spotlights.

Suddenly Angus was glad there were no ropes from the ceiling. His hands were shaking too much for a traditional pirate entrance.

Rindi took a deep breath. 'I'll try the non-pirate way first,' she said.

She went over to an elegant saleswoman in a green blazer.

'Excuse me,' said Rindi. 'Are these contraceptives for sale?'

The saleswoman looked Rindi up and down.

'They can be ordered,' she said, 'in lots of two hundred.'

'Any free samples?' asked Rindi.

'Not for kids,' said the woman, and turned away.

Rindi came back over to Angus. 'I tried,' she said. 'It'll have to be plan P.'

They swung into action.

Rindi took Imogen out of her stroller and Angus took an ice-cream out of his pocket and unwrapped it.

It was half melted. Perfect. He gave it to Imogen.

'What about mine?' wailed Leo.

Rindi gave Angus an alarmed look. Angus knew what she was thinking. If Leo threw a tantrum they were history.

Angus took another ice-cream out of his other pocket and gave it to Leo.

'Sorry,' said Rindi. 'I should've remembered you're an experienced parent.'

Angus reached into the stroller bag and pulled out Sidney the bear.

'Here goes,' he said.

'Cindy,' gurgled Imogen through a mouthful of melting ice-cream.

Angus put Sidney into Imogen's free hand, gently turned her around and pointed to where the saleswoman was chatting to her colleagues.

'Imogen take Sidney for walkies,' said Angus. 'Say hello to the green lady.'

'Walkies,' gurgled Imogen happily and waddled off towards the saleswoman, waving Sidney and leaving a trail of ice-cream.

'I want to go for a walk too,' said Leo. 'I want to find some snails.'

'Stay here,' said Angus, 'and guard the stroller. I'm depending on you.'

'OK,' said Leo. 'I'll get the snails later.'

Angus saw that Rindi was in position next to a display of diaphragms. He took his position next to a display of intra-uterine devices.

The saleswoman turned. Angus held his breath. Had she seen Imogen? No, she'd seen Angus. She was staring at him, puzzled. She took a step towards him.

Then Imogen reached her. First Sidney, then the ice-cream, made contact with the saleswoman's skirt. The saleswoman recoiled, horrified. Her colleagues stepped forward to help.

'A baby,' said the saleswoman, appalled.

'Cindy,' gurgled Imogen proudly.

Angus grabbed an intra-uterine device and tried to pull it off its board. It was a fiddly little plastic and metal thing and he realised it was fixed to the board with wire.

He couldn't get it off.

Angus glanced frantically over at Rindi and

saw that she was using her teeth. He tried to do the same, but he couldn't get his mouth in the right position.

One of the salesmen picked Imogen up. Her nappy burst open. The salesman put her down. Angus chewed frantically at the wire.

'Hey!'

The salesman had seen him.

'I've got one of each,' yelled Rindi. 'Let's go!'

Angus stopped gnawing and ran over to the saleswoman, who was wiping her skirt with Sidney and holding a giggling Imogen by the wrist.

He picked Imogen up and grabbed the sticky Sidney.

'Sorry,' he said and bolted for the stroller.

'Is this a play?' asked Leo as Angus plonked Imogen into her seat.

'No,' said Angus. 'Push.'

Angus pushed with all his strength but the bent wheel was dragging and he couldn't get any speed up.

After about three steps, a big hand grabbed his shoulder from behind.

'You're not going anywhere,' said a furious salesman.

Angus saw Rindi weaving through bemused onlookers like a pirate racing for the edge of the ship with a hot cannonball. She reached the exit.

'Rindi,' he yelled. 'Run.'

She stopped and looked back, turned towards the exit, then looked back again. Her shoulders slumped.

'Run,' yelled Angus. 'Run.'

But even as he was yelling, she was walking back.

'Let him go,' she yelled at the salesman and the other salespeople who were crowding round. 'I took them.'

She handed a diaphragm and an intra-uterine device to the salesman.

'One was for me,' said Angus.

'This is disgraceful,' said the saleswoman. 'These aren't toys, you know. They're sophisticated pieces of medical equipment that have to be fitted by trained doctors.' She glared at Angus and Rindi. 'Disgraceful.'

Rindi glared back at her.

'Perhaps you wouldn't think it was so disgraceful,' said Rindi angrily, 'if you were being taken to India next month and forced to marry a really old man. A twenty-two-year-old man your parents had chosen who you'd never even met. Perhaps then you'd do whatever you had to do to stop him making you pregnant, even if it meant stealing stuff.'

Rindi stopped, out of breath, eyes flashing.

She is brilliant, thought Angus.

There was a silence. Salespeople and customers at other stands were looking.

'We don't need this sort of publicity,' muttered the saleswoman. 'Get them out of here.'

One of the security guards escorted them out of the building.

When the security guard had warned them that if they went back in he'd call the police, and had gone back inside himself, Angus turned to Rindi.

'That was amazing,' he said. 'You're a genius. How did you think of all that? And the way you said it. You should be a professional actor. My mum could get you a part in her . . .'

He trailed off. Rindi wasn't looking at him proudly, or even modestly. She was looking at the ground and tears were dripping off her face.

Angus stared.

'She's a better pretender than Mum,' whispered Leo. 'Mum can't cry that good.'

Angus gently put his hand over Leo's mouth.

He looked again at the misery and desperation on Rindi's face and realised with a surge of horror that she wasn't acting.

14

'Mum,' said Angus, 'listen to me. Her parents are making her get married.'

'Outrageous,' said Mum, 'absolutely outrageous.' She stopped rummaging in the bottom of her wardrobe and stood up. 'How can a bolero jacket just vanish, it's outrageous.'

'Mum,' yelled Angus. 'She's just a kid.'

Mum stared at him.

Angus realised with a stab of panic that he'd never yelled at Mum before.

'Sorry,' he murmured, wondering what was going to happen now. When Number Two used to yell at Mum, she'd yell back at him for hours.

'Angus,' said Mum gently, 'what's happening to your friend sounds awful, but I just don't have time to think about it now because what's happening to me is pretty awful too. I've got to open a new shopping centre in an hour and I can't find my bolero jacket.'

Angus sighed.

It had been a wild hope, but he'd thought that she just might listen.

Sadly, he went into his room and got her bolero jacket.

'I borrowed it last week for the school play,' he said.

She stared at it, horrified. 'It's got skulls painted on it,' she said. 'And brown blobs.'

'It's parrot poo,' said Angus. 'I was a pirate in the play till I got chucked out.'

'How could you do this?' screeched Mum. 'It's Saturday morning. The wardrobe department at the studio is closed. What am I meant to wear?'

'Sorry,' said Angus.

'I'll have to make do with this,' said Mum. She dragged a dress out of the tangle of wire hangers.

'It suits you,' said Angus.

'No it doesn't,' said Mum. 'It shows up my wrinkles.' She stared into the mirror. 'I look like a prune. No wonder I had to bully Gavin into coming with me today.'

'You're just tired,' said Angus.

'Of course I am,' said Mum. 'I've got too many kids. I'm run off my feet in every scene. I told the writers three was enough, but no, along came Craig. They've no idea how exhausting it is acting with kids. Making things up when the little darlings forget their lines. Worrying the baby's going to throw up on you. I tried to warn them. Even a supermum, I said, can have too many kids.'

Angus took a deep breath and tried to keep his voice steady. Here, out of the blue, was a chance to have a serious talk to Mum about the facts of life.

'Sometimes,' he said hopefully, 'real life can be like TV, eh?'

Mum stared at him.

'Real-life mums,' he continued, 'can have too many kids as well, sometimes.'

She threw her arms round him and hugged his face into her dressing gown.

'Don't even think that,' she said. 'You're my real-life kids. I've never thought there were too many of you. I love you. I've never regretted having you for a moment.'

Angus closed his eyes and put his arms round Mum. Oh well, he thought wearily, it was worth a try.

He clung to her as hard as he could. Maybe things would get better. Maybe Mum would get too old to have any more babies. Ms Lowry had. Renee Stokes had asked her in class.

Angus felt Mum kissing his head. His insides started to feel warm and tingly. Then she held him at arm's length and gazed at him with soft eyes.

'I love my babies,' she said dreamily. 'All of them. If things turn out well with Gavin, I'll probably have another one.'

Suddenly Angus's insides weren't warm and tingly any more.

He stood there, numb. He was dimly aware of Mum kissing him on the nose and going into the bathroom.

Angus didn't move for a long time.

Then he looked down and saw that he was still holding the Bumface jacket. He could see his old tear stains smudging the skulls and parrot poo.

He thought of the future, full of babies.

All bawling their heads off.

Part of him wanted to bawl now, but he gritted his teeth and forced the tears back down.

It was too late.

His life was over.

All he could do now was try to save Rindi.

Part Three

15

Angus rang Rindi's front door bell and took a step back and tried to breathe slowly.

Use short words, he reminded himself. Cruel parents who force their daughter to get married before she's even in high school are probably violent too. They probably don't like people trying to persuade them to change their minds. You might not have long before they blow their tops and attack.

Angus glanced back to where Leo was minding Imogen at the front gate. The bent wheel was the main worry. If they had to run for it they'd probably have to ditch the stroller.

The door opened.

A woman smiled down at Angus. 'Hello,' she said.

Angus stared. If this was Rindi's mum she was quite a bit older than he'd expected. And she wasn't wearing Indian clothes, just a normal dress.

'I'm a friend of Rindi's,' blurted out Angus louder than he'd meant to. 'And I just want to say –'

'A friend of Rindi's,' said the woman, looking delighted. 'Come in, come in.' She saw Leo and Imogen at the gate and beckoned to them. 'Come in, all of you.'

Angus didn't know what to do. Leo was struggling to push the stroller down the path. Angus and the woman both went to help, and before Angus knew it they were wrestling the stroller into the house.

A man came into the hallway. He was wearing the longest shirt Angus had ever seen. He peered at the bent wheel on the stroller. 'That's been in the wars,' he said. 'I'll see if I can fix that for you.'

'A friend of Rindi's,' the woman whispered to the man, still looking pleased. 'From school.'

'I'm not actually from Rindi's school,' said Angus. 'I've come because I want to –'

'Rindi,' called the woman. 'A friend is here.'

Rindi appeared in a doorway. Angus could see she'd been crying. She stared at him, surprised.

'A friend to cheer us up,' said the woman.

'Not to cheer you up,' said Leo. 'To tell you off.'

'Go to bed,' yelled Imogen.

Rindi gave half a grin. 'Angus and Leo and

120

Imogen,' she said. 'My parents.' Her face fell. 'They think I can be cheered up.'

Angus saw that Rindi's dad, who was much older than any of his dads, was looking suddenly stern.

'Forgive Rindi,' he said. 'She is unhappy because her life must change.'

'We are all sad,' said Rindi's mum quietly. 'Our daughter is to be married and we will miss her very, very much.'

'That's why I've come,' said Angus. 'To –'

'We appreciate your concern,' said Rindi's dad. 'But this is a family matter.'

'No,' yelled Rindi. 'He's my friend. I want him to understand why he won't see me any more.'

Angus couldn't bear to look at her sad, tear-streaked face. He looked nervously at Imogen instead. She wasn't used to yelling. Apart from her own.

'Let's sit down and talk,' said Rindi's mum to Angus. 'Please have some tea and cake. Do you like cake?'

'Not as much as me,' said Leo.

While Rindi's mum poured lemonade for Leo and Imogen, and Rindi's dad took the stroller out to his shed, Rindi got Angus to help her make the tea.

She squeezed Angus's arm. 'Thanks for trying,' she said.

Angus watched her throw a handful of teabags into the pot without even counting them.

'I haven't finished yet,' he said.

Rindi's dad came back in with the stroller. The wheel was straight and spinning perfectly. Angus thanked him and as they all went into the lounge Angus wondered if Rindi had two dads, a cruel one and this nice one.

Once the tea was poured and Leo and Imogen had big mouthfuls of cake, Rindi's mum looked at Rindi's dad.

He nodded.

'We are sad,' said Rindi's mum, 'but we are also excited because Rindi's future husband Patel is arriving in Australia this evening to meet her. Usually this doesn't happen, but because Rindi is Australian as well as Indian, and we know how hard this is for her, we've arranged it.'

Angus glanced at Rindi. Her eyes were filling with tears again.

'I have known Patel's father for fifty-two years,' said Rindi's dad softly. 'As a young man he saved my life in a flood. Many other things we shared. We dreamed that one day our two families would be joined through marriage. When Patel was born, I celebrated with his family and hoped that my first child would be a girl.' Rindi's father gave a small smile. 'Rindi was eleven years arriving. She has always been stubborn.'

Angus passed Rindi a serviette under the coffee table so she could mop up her tears.

'Rindi's not stubborn,' said Leo. 'She's a pirate.'

'Rindi sad,' crooned Imogen. She threw a piece of cake and hit Rindi's dad on the head.

'Sorry,' said Angus, horrified.

'That's all right,' said Rindi's dad, brushing the crumbs off his shoulder. 'Rindi used to do the same thing.'

Angus looked at Rindi, hoping she'd smile. She didn't.

'If we lived in India,' said Rindi's mum, 'this arranged marriage would be quite normal. But it wouldn't happen until Rindi was sixteen or seventeen. Unfortunately we live here and Patel's family and Rindi's father think she's becoming too Australian. They think if she stays here much longer she won't be able to adjust to being an Indian wife.'

'I *am* Australian,' said Rindi through clenched teeth. 'I've been here since I was three.'

'She ignores my instructions,' said Rindi's dad quietly, 'and stays out after school.'

'That was my fault,' said Angus. 'She was meeting me. Well, she did once.'

He looked pleadingly at Rindi's dad.

Rindi's dad stared at the floor, not speaking.

'Patel's family want the wedding soon,' said Rindi's mum, her voice wavering. 'And then

Rindi will have to go and live with Patel's family in India.'

'But of course not have children,' said Rindi's dad. 'Not for several years.'

Rindi sat motionless, eyes closed. Angus wished he could go and put his arms round her.

'Can she still watch "The Simpsons"?' asked Leo.

Nobody answered.

'Eat my shorts,' shrieked Imogen.

Angus saw that Rindi's mum was close to tears. After a struggle she managed to smile. 'Patel is a wonderful young man,' she said. 'Listen to what he wrote to us.' She took a letter and some photos out of an envelope.

'I believe,' she read, 'that love can grow between a man and a woman until it is so strong that it will hold their children safe forever.'

Rindi's mum dabbed her eyes with a serviette and Angus felt his own eyes pricking. He blinked hard before Rindi noticed.

Suddenly Angus was confused. He hated what they were doing to her and he'd do everything he could to stop them. He'd even throw cake himself if it would help. But when he looked at Rindi's mum now, gazing with such concern at Rindi, he felt something else.

He felt jealous.

Stop it, he said to himself, this isn't helping Rindi.

To get his mind back on track, Angus looked at the photos of Patel. Angus had to admit he was handsome. Plus he had the look of a bloke who'd stick by his kids.

Angus stared at the photos for a long time.

'That's a good girl,' he heard Rindi's mum say softly to her. 'Dry your tears. See, your friend understands. You needn't have worried.'

Later, while Rindi's mum was lying down with a headache and Rindi's dad was playing snakes and ladders with Leo and Imogen, Angus helped Rindi wash up.

He squeezed her arm.

'Don't worry,' he whispered. 'I've had an idea.'

16

Angus opened his eyes and peered through the darkness at his chest of drawers.

No alarm clock.

Angus sighed. Imogen must have put it in the washing machine again. He found his watch and held it up in the chink of light between the curtains.

Ten twenty-five?

It couldn't be.

Rindi and her parents and Patel were arriving at eleven and he hadn't even told Mum they were coming yet.

He'd meant to each time Imogen had woken him and Mum up with her teething, but each time he'd been too tired to get the words out.

Angus struggled out of bed.

I don't know what's more exhausting, Angus thought as he dragged his clothes on. Being woken up in the night by a teething kid or a horde of hungry mice.

He remembered what Rindi's mum had said about Patel. How he only needed four hours sleep a night because he did meditation. Boy, thought Angus wearily, that'd be useful.

Angus checked that Imogen was still asleep and Leo was safely in front of the TV. Then he hurried into Mum's room.

Number Four wasn't there. Good, it was all going to plan so far.

'Mum,' he whispered urgently. 'Time to wake up.'

Sleepily she dragged the pillow off her head. 'It's Sunday,' she said. 'Go away.'

'Mum,' he said. 'You've got to get up.'

'Oh, that's right,' she groaned. 'Mother's Day. Tell you what. I'll look at the prezzie then have a bit more sleep, OK?'

Angus hesitated.

'Well?' she said, sitting up. 'Where is it?'

'Um,' he said, 'it's not here yet.'

'That's good,' she said, flopping back down. 'Wake me up when it arrives.'

'Mum,' said Angus, shaking her. 'I've invited some people over.'

'What?' she yelled, sitting up again. This time she reached over to the bedside table and switched on the lamp. Angus saw she had makeup smeared all over her face, and her hair looked like Sidney the bear's after he'd been in the clothes dryer.

Not so good.

If Patel saw her looking like that he almost certainly wouldn't fall in love with her and want to be the father of her future babies.

'It's OK,' Angus said to Mum. 'They won't be here for half an hour. You've got time to get ready.'

'Another lamington, Patel?' asked Mum.

'Not for me, thank you Marlene,' said Patel. 'They give me wind.'

'Patel suffers from stress,' said Rindi's dad to Mum, 'because although he's only twenty-two he's got a very responsible job.'

Rindi's mum and dad both smiled proudly.

Angus looked at Rindi and wondered why she was chewing her lamington with her mouth open. Then he realised it was so Patel wouldn't find her attractive.

'What do you do, Patel?' asked Mum.

'Computer salesman,' said Patel.

Angus swapped a look with Rindi. Mum and Patel were talking direct. This was good.

'Probably,' said Angus, 'the best computer salesman in India.'

Patel beamed with pleasure. 'I wouldn't quite say that,' he murmured, smoothing down his silk tie.

'One of the best,' murmured Rindi's dad.

Angus glanced at Mum to see if she was

impressed that Patel was wearing a suit even though it was Sunday morning. She wasn't even looking at him. She was scraping soggy rusk off her track pants.

'Would you like anything else to eat?' Angus asked the guests, hoping Imogen wouldn't throw any more rusks and put Patel off his appetite.

'No thanks,' said Rindi's mum and dad.

'I'd rather like another fried egg,' said Patel.

'Coming right up,' said Angus, handing him the platter and feeling very glad he'd decided to have a bit of a fry-up to show Patel how good Australian food was. A bloke wouldn't be tempted to move to a different country and start a family if he didn't like the food.

'Bacon?' asked Angus, offering him the other platter. 'Sausage? Fish cake?'

'Just the egg, thank you,' said Patel. 'Is this the salt shaker?'

'That,' said Angus, 'is Mum's Logie award. She got it for being the most popular actress in the whole of Australia in a television series or serial.'

Rindi's mum and dad looked impressed.

'How wonderful,' said Patel, looking at Mum admiringly.

'She's probably the most popular actress Australia's ever had,' said Rindi through a mouthful of lamington.

Mum pretended to be embarrassed. 'You're very sweet,' she said to Rindi. 'But I don't know why Angus put it on the table.' She turned to Angus. 'I like your new friend,' she said, winking at Rindi's mum and dad.

She could mean Patel, thought Angus hopefully. It's possible.

He handed Patel the salt and pepper shakers. 'The Prime Minister gave Mum those,' he said.

Patel looked impressed.

'He didn't really,' said Mum. 'I went to a charity lunch at his place and pinched them.'

Patel put them down. Rindi's mum and dad looked uncomfortable.

'Guess what, Mum,' said Angus hurriedly. 'Patel only needs four hours sleep a night.'

'Gee,' said Mum. She turned to Rindi. 'How do you feel about getting married so young, love?' she asked.

Rindi looked down at the floor. Angus could see she was suddenly close to tears. Mum, he thought wearily, you're not helping.

'We pray she'll get used to the idea,' said Rindi's dad.

'Eventually,' said Rindi's mum quietly.

'In India,' said Patel, 'arranged marriages are quite common. We believe two people will have a stronger marriage if their families work together to help them find love. We think arranged marriages are better than what happens here in

Australia. People falling in love and out of love. Having two or three or more marriages. And children from each. Terrible.'

Patel, thought Angus hopelessly, you're not helping either.

Mum was frowning at Patel. Angus saw Patel look away uncomfortably.

They weren't two people who were falling in love.

Oh well, thought Angus sadly. It was worth a try.

'It's a shame that Gavin my darling fiancé's not here,' said Mum, still frowning at Patel. 'He loves discussing social issues.'

Angus stared at Mum.

Fiancé?

'We're not officially engaged yet,' said Mum to Rindi's parents. She glanced at Angus.

'You may be interested to hear,' said Rindi's dad, 'that our own marriage was arranged. And twenty-six years later we are still happy, aren't we my dear?'

He looked at Rindi's mum, who smiled and nodded.

Angus had a wild idea. If things didn't work out between Mum and Number Four, perhaps Rindi's parents could help arrange a marriage for Mum. Find her a bloke who would stick around and help look after Leo and Imogen.

And me, thought Angus.

He felt a pang of longing and was tempted to ask Rindi's parents right away.

Then he remembered that this wasn't helping Rindi.

Mum had turned to her again. 'How do you feel about living in India?' she asked.

Angus could see Rindi was even closer to tears than before.

'My parents have a large and luxurious house,' said Patel. 'My mother will soon turn Rindi into a grown-up young woman. Then I will take her to art galleries and classical concerts and political meetings. My friends will be very impressed by her. I will be very proud.'

Angus wanted to leap across the table and give Patel a good shake. 'She's just a kid,' he wanted to scream.

But he didn't. Suddenly he realised it wasn't Patel's fault. Patel had probably been told since he was a kid that he was going to marry Rindi. And you couldn't blame him for liking her.

Angus looked Patel straight in the eye.

'Will you be playing pirates much?' he asked.

There was a stunned silence. Then all the adults laughed, including Mum.

Angus jumped to his feet. He grabbed Rindi's hand. 'Excuse us,' he said, steering her towards the door, 'Rindi's going to help me with some homework.'

In Angus's room, Rindi threw herself on the bed.

'Sorry,' said Angus. 'That was hopeless.'

'You tried,' said Rindi. 'I'll always be grateful for that.'

'I haven't finished yet,' said Angus.

Rindi blew her nose on his bedspread and sat up.

Angus looked at her. She was brave but was she brave enough?

'He's pretty concerned about what his friends are going to think of you,' he said.

'You can say that again,' said Rindi, scowling.

Angus told her his new plan.

17

There were no ropes hanging from the ceiling of the school corridor, so Angus had to do his pirate raid on foot.

I bet professional pirates do a lot of work on foot, he thought as he crept towards the pegs. On desert islands, for example, and in shopping centres and walking the plank.

Angus ducked low as he passed the classroom door. He could hear Ms Lowry's voice inside. 'Today's police visit,' she was saying, 'will be at eleven.'

Angus wondered if professional pirates ever felt fear. Probably not. But then professional pirates probably only did one bad thing at a time. I bet they'd be shaking like me, thought Angus, if they had to steal, lie and be late for school all on the same day.

Further down the corridor the staffroom door opened.

Angus flattened himself against the wall under the bags. Mr Nash came out of the staffroom reading a sheet of paper.

Please don't come this way, begged Angus silently. A girl's life will be ruined if you do.

Mr Nash went into the staff toilet.

Thank you, said Angus to Mr Nash's bladder.

With trembling hands, Angus lifted Russell Hinch's bag off its peg and unzipped it. He felt around inside. The bag was almost full. He could feel supermarket trolley wheels and car badges and bits of public phones. And right down the bottom at the back, another zip.

A secret pocket.

Angus opened the zip and squeezed his fingers inside.

There it was. Angus could feel its square plastic body and dangling keyring.

The Tamagotchi.

'Crime is up,' said the sergeant, 'in every Australian city.'

He wrote 'crime up' on the blackboard.

Never mind crime up, thought Angus, what about hand up? Surely an experienced Police School Visits Officer could see when a kid desperately wanted to say something?

Angus put his aching right arm down and his left one up.

Ms Lowry waved at him to put it down. He ignored her.

'Theft is up,' said the sergeant, 'more than any other crime.'

He wrote 'theft up more' on the blackboard.

Angus waved his arm frantically. He could see Rindi outside the door, peering anxiously into the classroom.

'Sergeant . . .' he said.

'Angus Solomon,' barked Ms Lowry. 'We do not interrupt visitors to the school in the middle of their talks.'

Russell Hinch sniggered. Several of his mates copied him.

'That's OK,' said the sergeant. 'I like audience feedback. What did you want to say, lad?'

Angus stood up.

'I want to confess,' he said.

The other kids stared. Ms Lowry gave him a warning look.

The sergeant grinned. 'A confession, eh?' he said. 'I get a few of those. What did you do? Cross the road when the light was red? Chase a cat up a tree?'

The other kids chortled, Russell Hinch louder than any of them.

'No,' said Angus. 'I stole Stacy Kruger's Tamagotchi.'

He held it up.

The classroom fell silent. Everyone stared at

the dangling Tamagotchi. Especially Russell Hinch, who looked to Angus as though he was having trouble breathing.

'My baby,' yelled Stacy. 'You've killed it.'

She snatched the Tamagotchi from Angus and collapsed back into her seat in tears, hugging it. Other girls crowded round, comforting her.

'Hang on,' said Julie Cheng, taking the Tamagotchi and looking at it closely. 'It's not dead. It's healthy. It's been really well looked after.'

Some of the boys started jeering at Angus and the rest stared at Russell Hinch, who was going bright pink. The girls were chatting animatedly. Ms Lowry and the sergeant were deep in conversation.

'Wait,' yelled Angus. 'I haven't finished.'

People looked at him and slowly the noise died down.

'I didn't steal it for me,' said Angus. He went over and opened the door. Rindi gave him a nervous smile as she came in. He took her hand and together they stood in front of the class.

Angus looked at each of the kids. They were all gaping. He could feel Rindi's hand trembling, but her face was calm and determined.

Even though Angus was about to give the most important acting performance of his life, he was amazed to find that he felt calm and determined too.

'I stole it for my girlfriend,' he said. 'She wanted it so I stole it for her.'

'I asked him to,' said Rindi.

Angus looked around the room again.

Every mouth was still open.

While Angus waited for the storm to break, he consoled himself with a thought.

At least Russell Hinch wasn't making kissy lips.

Rindi's parents didn't make kissy lips either. Their lips stayed thin and angry and moved non-stop as they told Angus and Rindi off for what seemed like hours.

'You're as much of a thief as he is,' said Rindi's dad to Rindi.

'You may well have ruined your life,' said Rindi's mum.

Or saved it, thought Angus.

He gave Rindi's hand a squeeze. Things were looking good. When they'd got back to Rindi's house the school had already phoned and Patel had already gone to his room to digest the news.

'And you,' said Rindi's dad to Angus. 'You seemed like such a grown-up boy.'

Angus tried to look miserable. It wasn't easy because what he was feeling was anxious and hopeful. He did his best and slowly the telling off came to an end.

Then Mum arrived and it started all over again.

'I'm really disappointed in you, Angus,' she said. 'Particularly tonight of all nights.'

Angus wondered what she meant, but before he could think about it much, Patel came into the room.

He looked grim.

Angus glanced at Rindi. She was looking at Patel without flinching.

Please, thought Angus. Please let him be disgusted with her for being a thief. Please let him be scared that his friends will have kittens if he marries her. Then, with a bit of luck, word will get round and all the other blokes in India will feel the same way.

Patel cleared his throat. Rindi's parents stood up.

'I have thought carefully about the incident,' said Patel, 'and I have decided that I will return to India tomorrow as planned and that the wedding will go ahead next month as planned.'

Angus felt Rindi stiffen next to him.

He wanted to grab Patel and yell 'she's a thief, you dope, what about your friends?' but he was paralysed with dismay.

'Rindi is a child,' said Patel, 'and childhood is the time for foolish pranks. Better she get that nonsense out of her system now because when we're married she will be a grown-up and there will be no more games.'

Rindi was motionless next to Angus, but he could hear tiny sobs deep inside her.

'Thank you for being so understanding, Patel,' said Rindi's dad. 'You are your father's son.'

Angus saw that Rindi's mum was gripping the back of a chair so tightly her knuckles were white.

Patel smiled. He turned to Angus. 'In my family,' he said, 'you would be punished severely for stealing. Australia is different, I understand that. But I will be asking Rindi's parents to make sure she does not see you again.'

All the way home, Angus stared out of the car window into the dusk. He stared at shops. He stared at trees. He stared at traffic light control boxes. He stared so he wouldn't have to remember the look Rindi gave him as he left.

Her eyes, dark and defeated.

It didn't work, the staring. All he could think of was how when he'd first met Rindi she'd had more energy than Bumface and now, a week later, she had the look of a person who was drowning.

'Poor Rindi,' said Mum, but Angus could tell Mum's mind was on other things. Shopping centres probably.

There must be something else I can do, thought Angus desperately. Something.

Then, as he was getting out of the car, an even more desperate thought hit him. 'Leo and Imogen,' he gasped in panic, grabbing Mum. 'I forgot to pick them up.'

'I did it,' said Mum. 'When the school rang, I left work early. We'd planned to finish early anyway, tonight being a special night.'

'What do you mean?' asked Angus when he could speak again.

Mum smiled and opened the front door. A loud cheer rang out. Angus blinked. The house was full of people, drinking and laughing.

Mum led him into the noisy crowd. Number Four appeared, took a swig from a bottle of champagne and gave Mum a kiss. There was another big cheer.

'What's going on?' said Angus.

'It's a party,' said Mum. 'An engagement party.' She gave Number Four a kiss in return. 'Me and Gavin are getting married.'

The rest of the evening was a blur for Angus.

Leo ate half a box of chocolates and was sick over Number Four's shoes.

People from Mum's TV family kept congratulating Angus and asking him when the wedding was. Angus was so dazed he didn't always know if they meant Mum's or Rindi's.

Then, while Angus was in Imogen's room changing her nappy and watching Number Four dance in the corner with a production assistant, Mum's TV husband lurched in.

'G'day, young Angus,' he said. 'Lookin' forward to having a few more little brothers and sisters?'

Angus smiled weakly.

'I love weddings,' continued Mum's TV husband. 'There'd be less strife in the world if there were more weddings.'

That's when Angus had the idea. It hit him so suddenly and so hard that he dropped the talc.

'Oops,' said Mum's TV husband.

'Oops,' said Imogen.

Oops nothing, thought Angus, insides tingling with excitement and fear. Even Bumface would drop the talc if he had an idea like this.

18

'Rindi,' said Angus. 'Will you marry me?'

Rindi stared at him, stunned.

Angus shuffled his feet awkwardly. 'Sorry,' he said. 'I know this is a bit sudden.'

A truck roared past, leaving them standing in a cloud of fumes.

He hoped Rindi would understand. Normally he'd have chosen somewhere a bit more romantic than a busy street corner on the way home from school. A beach at dawn, say, or a submarine at sunset.

Angus glanced down the street to the bus shelter where he'd made Leo and Imogen wait. He could see they'd almost finished their ice-creams. Then he peered anxiously down Rindi's street, desperately hoping the corner he and Rindi were standing on wasn't visible from her house.

He looked at Rindi. She still wasn't saying anything.

Shock probably.

'If I marry you,' he said gently, 'Patel won't be able to.'

Her face lit up. Then it clouded over. 'Angus,' she said, 'we've only known each other for eight days.'

'You've only known Patel for one and a half days,' said Angus. 'Plus he's old enough to be your much older brother. I reckon love could grow between us. We both like pirates.'

Rindi looked at him and suddenly her eyes were glowing like he hadn't seen them do for days. 'And each other,' she said softly.

Angus suddenly felt an urgent need to look at his feet.

But only because she was right.

Rindi sighed. 'We're too young,' she said. 'People can't get married in Australia at our age. It's against the law.'

'It doesn't have to be legal,' said Angus. 'Your parents reckon Patel's really religious. If we get married in the eyes of God, that'll be enough to put him off.'

Rindi thought about this and nodded slowly. 'But who'd marry us?' she said.

Angus reached into his school bag and pulled out a TV magazine. He pointed to the article he'd been staring at most of the day at school.

'There's a TV show where people get married live on air,' he said. 'They broadcast it from the studio next to Mum's on Thursday nights.'

'My parents watch it sometimes,' said Rindi, taking the magazine.

'I can get us into the studio,' said Angus. 'If we stand where nobody can see us, and listen to the minister, and say "I do" at the right moment, and mean it, I reckon that'll make us married in the eyes of God.'

Rindi stared at him, then back at the magazine.

While she read the article, Angus looked down the street at Leo and Imogen. They'd finished their ice-creams. Frantically he signalled to them to stay where they were and be patient.

When he turned back to Rindi, she was gazing at him, her face troubled.

'Angus,' she said. 'You're the best friend I've ever had, but do you really want to marry me?'

Angus took a deep breath. He'd been asking himself that question all day. The answer wasn't simple. If they had different parents, he and Rindi would probably just stay best friends.

But they didn't.

Rindi's parents had forgotten she was just a kid.

His mum had forgotten how to have a proper marriage that lasted.

Plus there was more.

Angus couldn't put it exactly into words. It

was a feeling he had when he thought of Rindi giving a pirate yell or biting an intra-uterine device off a display board.

A feeling he'd never had before.

He realised Rindi was still looking at him, her face troubled.

He realised he was grinning.

'Yes,' he said, 'I do want to marry you. Do you want to marry me?'

Rindi gave the biggest smile he'd ever seen her give.

'Yes,' she said.

Angus laid his wedding suit out on his bed and gave a satisfied sigh.

Mum's bolero jacket was looking great now he'd painted over the skulls in silver and done the parrot poo in gold.

And Number Two's old black jeans looked pretty good too, cut off at the knee with a yellow stripe sewn down each side and Number Three's green silk scarf for a belt.

It was great having dads who left clothes behind when they moved on.

Angus gave a final polish to the purple boots that the production assistant had left in Imogen's room. They'd cleaned up really well. A good rub with detergent and almost all of Imogen's crayon marks had come off.

A pretty top wedding outfit, thought Angus

happily, seeing that we only decided to get married twenty-seven hours ago.

The phone rang.

Angus assumed it would be Mum saying she'd be late, but it was Rindi.

'I've got to be quick,' she whispered. 'Mum and Dad are watching the news. What sort of thing are you wearing tomorrow night?'

'Pirate,' said Angus.

There was a silence at the other end.

'All right,' said Rindi after a bit, 'I will too.'

Angus grinned.

'Except,' continued Rindi, 'I haven't really got anything pirate.'

'Don't worry,' said Angus, 'there's a wardrobe department at the TV station. They've got heaps of stuff.'

There was another silence.

'Angus,' said Rindi. 'Do you think we can do it?'

'Yes,' said Angus. 'We both want to, so nothing can stop us.'

19

'Just a minute,' said the security guard at the TV station gate. 'Where do you think you're going?'

Angus looked up at him pleadingly and pointed to Imogen's mouth, which looked a bit swollen due to the large number of jelly babies he'd squeezed into it.

'My sister's teething,' he said. 'Our mum works here.'

'She's a TV star,' said Leo through his own mouthful of jelly babies.

The security guard looked hard at Angus. 'Marlene Solomon's kids,' he said. 'Haven't seen you for yonks.' He looked at Rindi. 'Don't remember you. Are you a member of the family?'

Angus said 'yes' before Leo could say anything about her being his future sister-in-law.

The security guard slapped a security sticker on the stroller. 'I'll ring your mum,' he said.

'It's OK,' said Angus hurriedly. 'No need to disturb her. I know where to find her.'

The security guard looked doubtful, but at that moment three buses arrived carrying the studio audience for the wedding show.

'Don't get lost,' said the security guard.

'I won't,' said Angus as he pushed the stroller across the carpark.

He didn't. He knew exactly where the wardrobe department was. When they got there, they all hid outside the door behind a big wooden hamburger from the morning cartoon show until Angus saw the wardrobe assistants hurrying off to the studio.

'OK,' he said to Rindi. 'Be quick.'

Angus watched Rindi disappear among the racks of costumes and felt a stab of concern. Perhaps he should be going with her. Except he was pretty sure grooms weren't meant to help brides get dressed for the wedding.

Angus took Mum's video camera out of the stroller bag and handed it to Leo. 'Do you remember what I told you?' he said.

Leo nodded. 'Lens cap off and don't wobble,' he recited, 'because the tape's going all the way to Indooroopilly.'

'India,' said Angus.

'That's what I meant,' said Leo.

Angus glanced anxiously at the entrance to the wardrobe department. No sign of Rindi.

Don't panic, he thought, you haven't got changed yourself yet.

Imogen swallowed the last of her mouthful of jelly babies just as Angus finished putting his pirate outfit on.

'Bumface Gussy,' she giggled.

'Stop it,' said Leo sternly. 'He's getting married.'

Imogen stopped giggling and Angus realised someone was standing behind him.

He turned.

It was Rindi. She was wearing a red dress that cascaded in layers all the way to the floor. From her ears hung silver earrings in the shape of cutlasses. On her head was a sparkling turban covered with plastic oranges, apples, lemons and bananas.

Angus blinked.

He didn't know what to say.

He'd never seen a girl looking so beautiful, and he didn't even particularly like fruit.

'You look fantastic,' he whispered.

'Even our mum's never looked that fantastic,' said Leo.

'Thanks,' said Rindi. 'I picked a long dress because I've got a big scab on one of my knees.'

Getting into the studio was a bit harder than Angus had planned.

He knew there was a door up near the roof

that led onto the lighting walkway, and he knew it was never locked because it was also the fire escape for the studio control room. Mum had given him a tour of the studio once on his birthday.

But she hadn't told him how to get up to the door.

'I think we're lost,' said Rindi as they climbed yet another flight of stairs.

Angus was too puffed to answer. He shifted Imogen to his other shoulder and pointed. Up ahead was a door marked Do Not Open When Studio On Air.

Angus opened it and they went inside.

Far below Angus could see the faces of the studio audience bright under the lights. Camera operators slowly steered their big cameras across the studio floor. The set was made up of big flat painted panels propped up all over the place to make the studio look like a church.

A floor manager called for silence as a commercial break came to an end.

'Are we going to do it up here?' whispered Rindi.

'No,' replied Angus. 'Too risky. If anyone looks up they can see us. We'll go down there into that corner behind the set.'

It was a slow climb down. The metal stairs were so steep they were almost like a ladder and Angus's hands were so sweaty he almost couldn't grip the handrail.

Halfway down Leo nearly dropped the video camera and Angus nearly dropped Imogen as he grabbed it.

'Bouncy Bumface,' gurgled Imogen, and Angus had to quickly stuff some more jelly babies into her mouth. Luckily the studio organ was playing and nobody seemed to have heard. Angus gave silent thanks to God, who he assumed was in the studio somewhere for the wedding, that 'Here Comes the Bride' was such a noisy tune.

They made it down to the back corner of the studio just in time. Angus could hear, on the other side of the set, the studio minister starting to ask the groom if he'd take the bride to be his wife.

Angus shifted Imogen to his other shoulder, signalled to Leo to start videoing, and murmured his own name and Rindi's when the minister said the groom's and the bride's.

Then he took Rindi's hand and looked into her shining eyes.

'I do,' he whispered.

Rindi took a deep wobbly breath and for a second Angus thought she was going to burst into tears. Perhaps she knocked her scab off on the ladder, he thought, concerned.

She didn't cry. She murmured her name and

his at exactly the right spots and looked into his eyes and whispered 'I do.'

Angus felt a lump in his throat. It couldn't be a jelly baby because he hadn't had any.

'You may kiss the bride,' said the minister's voice.

Angus looked awkwardly at the floor and felt his face getting hot. He'd forgotten about this bit. Did grooms kiss brides in arranged marriages? He was still trying to decide when he felt Rindi's lips against his cheek.

He pressed his lips to her cheek and she grinned and threw a handful of confetti into the air above their heads.

On the other side of the set, the studio audience erupted into cheers, whistles and applause. Angus's chest felt like it was going to burst with happiness.

They'd done it.

They were married.

But it wasn't Angus's chest that burst, it was Imogen's nappy.

By the time Angus felt the warm liquid running down his arm, there was already a narrow stream trickling across the floor towards Leo. At that moment Leo lunged forward to video a cockroach scampering across the studio floor.

Angus opened his mouth to yell a warning, but it was too late. Leo trod in the wee. His foot skidded out from under him. He staggered back and crashed into the set.

Leo and a huge section of the set teetered, rocked towards Angus, and then rocked away from his clutching hand and crashed to the floor.

Angus blinked. The last bits of confetti fluttered past his face. Staring at him were three hundred shocked audience members, four TV cameras and another happy couple.

20

Angus didn't realise just how bad things were until he got to school the next day.

Up until then, his wedding hadn't seemed that big a disaster, considering.

Once the studio audience had got over their shock, they'd laughed and clapped. The crew had been pretty amused too, which had been a big relief to Angus. The end titles must have been rolling by the time Leo and the set had fallen over.

The floor manager took Angus and the others into the next studio to find Mum, but she'd gone, so he put them in a taxi.

Mum wasn't at home either. Just Dad, rummaging through drawers looking for money. He left, embarrassed at being sprung. Mum got home very late and wasn't in a mood to talk, but Angus gleaned that it was her wedding she was upset about and not his.

Phew.

It was Rindi he was worried about.

When they'd got to Rindi's place in the taxi, Angus had wanted to go inside with her.

'I'm your husband,' he'd said. 'I should come in and tell them with you.'

She'd squeezed his arm. 'No. It'll be very ugly. Best get the little kids home.'

Angus had tried to persuade her but she'd been firm.

Now, getting close to school, his chest felt tight as he remembered his last sight of her from the taxi. Alone under a streetlight, waving, his Bumface jacket round her shoulders. Suddenly she'd looked like a little kid herself, even though she was clutching the video of her wedding.

Angus had rung her loads of times right up until he finally fell asleep, and loads more when he got up, but her phone had been busy every time.

I'll ring her from the staffroom, he thought as he went in the school gate. I'll tell Mr Nash it's a family emergency, which is true.

Angus stopped.

What was going on?

Every kid in the playground was standing still.

Staring at him.

Renee Stokes came over with some of the

other girls. 'I think that was so beautiful,' said Renee passionately, 'what you did last night.'

The other girls started telling him that they thought it was beautiful too. Some of the boys started doing kissy lips and a couple yelled things out. Stuff about honeymoons and wedding cake. Russell Hinch just stared at Angus as if he still couldn't believe it.

Angus didn't take much of it in.

Panic roared in his ears.

He and Rindi must have gone to air. They must have been on TV. Half the country must have seen them standing side by side in their wedding outfits, covered in confetti.

Angus could see the magazine headlines. 'Soapie Supermum's Neglected Child Weds.' The viewers would blame Mum. They'd turn off in their millions. Mum would get the sack. She'd be furious.

If Rindi's parents throw her out, Angus thought desperately, she'll have to come and live with me at Dad's. When she meets Pirate Jim she'll probably wish she was with Patel.

At least there were no lessons. When Angus stumbled into class he discovered that everyone was off painting scenery for the school play and writing 'Tonite' across all the posters.

He was able to make lots of calls, to Mum and to Rindi. He didn't get through to either of them.

As soon as the bell went at the end of the afternoon, Angus sprinted over to the infants and grabbed Leo.

'Everyone saw you and your wife on TV,' said Leo. 'It ruined my show and tell.'

Angus dragged Leo to the childcare centre, picked up Imogen and headed for home as fast as he could.

His insides were aching with anxiety.

'Are you all right?' asked Leo.

'I'm fine,' Angus muttered, pushing the stroller harder.

'Bumpy Bumface,' yelled Imogen.

Leo leant forward and put his lips next to Imogen's ear. 'Married life doesn't agree with him,' he whispered.

When Angus got home he was horrified to find Mum was already there. With tear-swollen eyes. The network must have fired her on the spot.

'Mum,' he said, anguished. 'About last night. I'm sorry. I didn't think.'

She looked at him with a vague expression and blew her nose on a tissue. 'Last night?' she said. Then she gave a half-smile. 'Oh, right, you and your friend on the wedding show. The network loved it. Best comedy ending to the show ever, they were saying today.'

Angus stared at Mum, trying to take in what he was hearing.

'I'm a bit cross they didn't tell me they were going to use you,' said Mum as she poured herself a drink. 'I am your mother, after all. That publicity department needs a boot up the bum. I'll have a word to them when I haven't got so much on my mind.'

'You mean,' stammered Angus, 'you haven't been dumped by the network?'

Mum looked at him as if he was mad. 'Not by the network, no.' She paused and stared into her drink. 'By Gavin maybe. Depends if the gossip I've been hearing today is true or not. About him and a certain production assistant.'

Angus realised Mum was holding one of his purple pirate boots. She flung it angrily to the floor.

The phone rang.

'Can you get it, darling?' muttered Mum, 'I'm in a big hurry.'

It was Rindi.

Her voice was so quiet and tearful Angus almost didn't recognise it.

'I have to be really quick,' she said. 'I'm at the airport. They're taking me to India tonight. The wedding's been brought forward to next week.'

Rindi's voice dissolved into sobs. Angus held onto the wall. 'But they can't,' he yelled into the phone. 'We're married.'

'They said it was just a stupid game and it

doesn't change anything,' sobbed Rindi. 'Oh no, they're coming. They've seen me. Angus, thank you. I'll never forget you. I'll never . . .'

The phone went dead.

'Rindi,' yelled Angus. 'Rindi!'

She was gone.

'Mum,' yelled Angus, 'quick.'

He sprinted out of the kitchen. If they drove to the airport as fast as they could, they might just be in time to alert airport security and get them to talk Rindi's parents out of the whole idea . . .

Angus realised he could hear Mum's car backing out of the driveway.

'Wait,' he screamed.

He heard Mum drive off.

Leo was standing at the front door holding a note. 'She said she'll see us at the school play,' he announced. He gave Angus the note and headed back to the TV.

Angus read the note. 'Gone to have things out with Gavin,' it said. 'See you at the school play. Leo's dad will pick you all up and take you there. Break a leg.'

Angus stared at the scrawly handwriting.

Break a leg.

I don't believe it, he thought. She thinks I'm still in the school play. I told her I'd been dumped and she's forgotten. Just like she's forgotten about Rindi. She thought we went on the wedding show for her publicity . . .

Angus leant against the wall. He saw that his hands were shaking. It's just exhaustion, he thought dully.

But he knew it wasn't.

It was something much more painful.

It was his body's way of telling him that his parents didn't care about him.

Angus felt sobs coming up from deep inside him but he forced them back down.

He grabbed Imogen's jacket off the hall peg. If we leave now, he thought wildly, and get a train and then an airport bus . . .

It was no good.

It would take hours.

Too long, anyway.

Angus slid down the wall until he was sitting on the floor.

What would Bumface do?

How would Bumface save Rindi?

He sat for a long time staring into the gloom, and by the time Number Two phoned to say he couldn't pick them up, Angus knew.

21

'Why aren't we dressed as pirates?' asked Leo.

'Shhhh,' said Angus.

'Gussy shooshy,' chortled Imogen.

Angus put his hand over her mouth. They'd got this far without being sprung. It would be tragic if they were caught now.

'Everyone else is dressed as pirates,' said Leo.

Angus took his hand off Imogen's mouth and put it over Leo's.

He peeked through the curtains at the back of the stage. Leo was right. The school hall was packed and every single member of the audience was in pirate costume. Angus could see kid pirates and parent pirates and teacher pirates and grandparent pirates and programme-seller pirates.

Angus blinked. There was Dad, near the front, wearing a Pirate Jim costume. And squeezing his way along the same row towards his seat,

Number Two, wearing the outfit he wore in *The Pirates of Penzance*. And just behind him, Number Three, wearing a leather waistcoat and an orange silk scarf.

Even Mum in the front row was wearing one of the cardboard pirate hats the Year Fours had made to give away with the programmes.

Mum was turning and mouthing something crossly at Number Two, who was shaking his head and mouthing something crossly back at her.

Angus sighed. Doing this would be easier if the family wasn't there, but he didn't have a choice.

Rindi's future was at stake.

Angus took a deep breath, shifted Imogen to his other shoulder, took Leo by the hand and stepped through the curtain onto the stage.

Stacy Kruger and Russell Hinch were doing their scene where Xena tells Blackheart she won't go with him to the pirate ball unless he gives back her brother's ears.

Stacy stopped mid-speech and stared. 'Angus,' she said, 'what are you doing here?

Russell Hinch spun round and gaped.

Angus stepped past them both and went to the front of the stage. Even with the lights in his eyes he could see the shock and puzzlement on the faces of the audience.

'Ladies and gentlemen,' he said as loudly as

he could. His throat was suddenly dry and a bit croaky. 'I'm sorry to bust into the play like this, but I need your help. It's urgent. Even as I speak, a girl is being flown to India against her will to marry someone much too old for her. I need your help to save her. She's just a kid.'

Angus was aware of footsteps behind him. He glanced over his shoulder. The entire cast was on the stage behind him, wide-eyed.

Angus turned back to the audience. There was a hum now as people whispered and murmured to each other.

'We need to contact the airline and get the plane to turn back,' continued Angus. 'If we can't do that we need to arrange for someone to meet the plane over there. Does anyone know any child welfare people in India?'

Angus strained to hear if anyone in the audience was saying yes. It was hopeless. The audience were all talking to each other. Some of them looked pretty concerned, but Angus couldn't hear a thing in the hubbub.

Except for one voice, behind him, shouting, 'Let me through.'

Ms Lowry.

Angus turned. Ms Lowry was striding towards him, scattering cast members, her eyes wide with fury.

She grabbed Angus by the neck of his T-shirt. 'Angus Solomon, how dare you ruin my play,' she hissed. 'Of all the childish, immature, irresponsible . . .'

For a second Angus didn't understand why the lights and the people and the scenery were all wobbling and going blurred. Then he realised Ms Lowry was shaking him. He hung on to Imogen as tightly as he could.

Another voice rang out close to Angus's ear. 'Stop that.'

It was Mum.

Mum was on stage next to him. She pulled him away from Ms Lowry and then turned to the audience. Angus saw a look in Mum's eyes he hadn't seen since he was a little kid and she was on stage in *No Sex Please, We're British*.

'My son,' said Mum, 'is not childish, he is not immature and he is not irresponsible.'

Angus stared, stunned, as she paused and swept the audience with her gaze. People had stopped talking and were watching her agog.

'My son,' she continued, pointing dramatically to Angus, 'helps look after his younger brother and sister with a maturity that I can only describe as truly adult. I trust him as if he was their parent. Hardly childish, immature or irresponsible, I think you'll agree.'

She took off her pirate hat and tossed back her hair.

Angus opened his mouth to remind everyone

about Rindi, but another voice was already ringing out.

'As one of their parents,' the voice boomed, 'I would like to add something.'

Angus blinked. Number Two was striding onto the stage.

Number Two took Leo's hand and stepped in front of Mum. As the audience gazed up at him, magnificent in his gold-sequinned pirate coat and three-cornered fur-trimmed pirate hat, he seemed to grow visibly.

'In our family,' he boomed, 'we pride ourselves on our maturity and responsibility. These qualities flow through our veins like the blood of life itself. My own son Leo embodies these qualities in every cell of his being.'

Leo, who'd been looking shocked, started to glow with pleasure. Number Two pointed dramatically to Angus.

'I will not,' he boomed, 'hear any member of my family impugned for lack of maturity or responsibility.'

Angus opened his mouth again, but someone else was aready speaking.

'Nor will I,' Number Three was saying as he clambered onto the stage. He took Imogen from Angus and stepped into the spotlight with her. 'My daughter is just as mature and responsible as any of them, and if anyone is looking for a father and daughter modelling duo . . .'

'Or,' said another voice, 'a father and son pirate-story-writing team . . .'

Angus realised Dad was standing right next to him.

'Angus may look young,' Dad continued, 'but he's got the imagination of a man three times his age.' He gave the audience the sincere expression Angus remembered from when Dad used to play the priest in a sit-com.

Chaos broke out.

Mum, Ms Lowry, Number Two, Number Three and Dad were all trying to speak at once. Audience members were shouting for their money back. Russell Hinch was yelling threats at Angus.

None of them, Angus realised, was worrying about Rindi.

He was the only one.

And he wasn't enough.

'Stop,' screamed Angus. 'I can't do it on my own.'

Nobody was listening.

Angus felt his chest start to shudder, and even though he was on stage in public with everyone watching and Russell Hinch only half a metre away, this time he couldn't stop the huge, painful sobs from shaking his whole body.

Slowly everyone stopped shouting. The hall fell silent. Everyone stared at Angus.

'I'm not a parent', he said, 'and I'm not an adult.'

The sobs were tearing his chest but it felt so good not to be acting.

Angus turned to Mum and Dad, who looked watery and indistinct through his tears. The sobs made it hard to speak but he managed to get the words out.

'Mum,' he pleaded, 'Dad, I'm just a kid.'

Nobody moved.

Nobody spoke.

They all just stared at him.

Angus said it again so everyone would understand.

'I'm just a kid.'

22

Angus sat staring gloomily out the living room window.

He should be having fun, he knew that. It was the school holidays, Leo was at the zoo with Number Two, Imogen was doing a nappy commercial with Number Three, and Mum had given Angus twenty dollars to spend on himself.

He didn't care.

He couldn't stop thinking about Rindi.

'You won't feel so sad,' Mum had said, 'as time passes. Look at me. I'm already getting over Gavin dumping me. Time heals everything.'

She was wrong. Two weeks had passed and Angus still felt a searing jolt of sadness when he opened his eyes each morning.

It wasn't fair.

Rindi's whole life, taken away.

Sure, I've got problems too, thought Angus, staring out the window. Mum'll probably find more blokes. She'll probably have more babies for me to look after. But compared to Rindi, I'm lucky.

Angus sighed. He didn't feel very lucky.

The door bell rang.

If that's Dad, thought Angus wearily, wanting more Pirate Jim story ideas, I'll tell him I've got the flu.

It was the postman.

'Parcel for Angus Solomon,' he said cheerily. He looked at Angus's face. 'Has someone died?'

Angus shook his head. 'Kidnapped,' he said.

The parcel was from India.

Angus could hardly breathe as he tore at the paper. He tried to think of good things it might be, but he could only think of bad things.

A piece of wedding cake.

A book about youth crime from Patel.

His Bumface jacket, returned by someone who'd found it in a rubbish bin at Calcutta airport.

He got the paper off.

It was a video cassette.

Angus's hands were shaking so much he could hardly get it into the video player. He stared at the TV screen. Fuzzy, wobbly pictures. He couldn't make out what it was at first. It looked like a home video shot by someone with worse camera skills than Leo.

Then, with a gasp, he realised.

It was Rindi's wedding video.

There she was, wearing a floaty, flowing robe that was very different from her real wedding dress. And a kind of shawl over her head and gold chains across her forehead and it even looked like she had a nose ring.

Angus squinted to see the details in the blurred images.

She seemed to be sitting on a sort of throne in a big tent. Angus caught glimpses of her parents and lots of other wedding guests. Then someone sat down on another throne next to her.

It was Patel.

Angus hit the pause button and looked away. Suddenly he wasn't sure if he wanted to see any more.

I must, he thought, I owe it to Rindi. She's suffered this, the least I can do is watch.

With a dull, sick feeling, Angus took the video off pause.

On the ground in front of Rindi and Patel, a small bonfire seemed to be burning. Probably Rindi's books and favourite things, thought Angus angrily.

A voice started chanting in another language. It went on for a long time. Angus went over to the screen so he could have a closer look at the expression on Rindi's face.

It was very sad.

Angus reached for the remote. I'll watch the rest tomorrow, he thought. Or next month.

Then Rindi stood up. There was something about the startled look Patel gave her that kept Angus watching.

Rindi pulled her robe off.

Angus stared. Underneath she was wearing the Bumface jacket.

She started running. Whoever was holding the camera was thrown into a panic, and for a while all Angus could see was the roof of the tent. Then Rindi was in shot again, snatching stuff off what looked like a long food table.

People were grabbing at her, but she wriggled away from them.

'Go,' someone was screaming. 'Go.'

Angus realised it was him.

On the screen, Rindi was climbing up a tentpole. She grabbed a rope and swung high over the shouting, arm-waving guests, pelting them with food. Patel, screaming at her in a rage, got a faceful of something gooey.

The tape ended.

Angus stared at the blank screen in delirious, joyful shock. Then he watched the tape again. And again. And again.

Each time, as he laughed and danced around and yelled encouragement to Rindi, a tiny nagging thought got slowly bigger.

What had happened next?

Had Rindi been dragged back to the throne and married with ropes round her?

Angus sat down, not feeling like dancing any more. Then he saw there was a note tucked in the video box.

'Dear Angus,' it said. 'They had me examined by a psychiatrist. He told them I'm not mental, just a naughty girl. Now everyone's beginning to think the wedding wasn't such a good idea, including my parents and the caterers. Everyone's saying I'm too Australian to be an Indian wife. See you soon, love Mrs Bumface.'

Angus put the tape back on and was still watching it and grinning when Dad walked in.

'Dad,' he said, startled. 'What are you doing here? I thought you were busy writing your book.'

Dad sat next to Angus on the settee.

'Turn the TV off,' he said, 'I've got something important I want to say to you.'

Angus turned the TV off. He looked at Dad warily. Usually when Dad had something important to say it involved borrowing money from Mum.

'I've been thinking since the school play,' said Dad quietly. 'I've been thinking how I haven't been a very good father to you.'

He put his arms round Angus and hugged him.

Angus hugged him back, tingling with pleasure and surprise.

'I've been thinking,' continued Dad, 'about what you said at the school play, and I can see now that me and Mum haven't been fair to you. The way we've expected you to be a grown-up all the time, that hasn't been fair to you at all. So I've decided that things are going to change.'

Angus's head was spinning. It was what he'd always dreamed of but had never dared actually hope for.

Dad was going to start being a dad.

Angus had wonderful visions of Dad taking him to the zoo. Dad doing a commercial with him. Dad playing pirates with him.

Then he realised that Dad was holding money out to him.

'A grown-up deserves grown-up pay, even if he is only little,' said Dad. 'I've decided that as you do almost all the work looking after Leo and Imogen, you should have most of the money Mum pays me to look after them. And as you've got quite a few more years of child-minding ahead of you, there'll be lots more where this came from.'

He pushed the notes into Angus's hand.

Angus stared at them, speechless with disappointment.

'It's OK,' said Dad. 'You don't have to say

anything. I know this is probably a bit overwhelming.'

Angus struggled to speak.

What could he say that he hadn't already said at the school play?

'There is just one other thing,' said Dad. 'I'm really short of cash at the moment, so I was wondering if I could borrow this first lot back, just for a bit.'

He slid the notes out of Angus's hand.

Angus didn't stop him.

He couldn't, he was too weak with despair.

'Good on you,' said Dad, gripping Angus by the shoulders. 'My Mr Reliable.'

Angus was still watching Rindi's tape, deep in thought, when Mum walked in.

'Mum,' he said, startled. 'It's only two o'clock. What are you doing home?'

She sat next to him on the settee.

'Turn the TV off,' she said, 'I've got some big news.'

Angus turned the TV off. He looked at Mum anxiously. The last time she'd said that, it was to tell him Dad was leaving.

Angus prepared himself for the worst.

'I'm out of the series,' said Mum.

Angus stared, panic rising. This *was* the worst.

'Today?' he stammered. 'Just like that? For good?'

Mum nodded.

Angus felt sick with shock.

Then he had a thought that made him feel even sicker.

There must have been a journalist at the school play. A magazine must have done a story about what happened. '"I'm Just a Kid" Sobs Star's Neglected Son.'

It must be his fault.

Angus prayed it wasn't.

'Why?' he croaked. 'Why are you leaving the series?'

Mum frowned. 'I'm pregnant,' she said.

Angus felt the last drops of joy trickle out of his life.

If only she could have waited just a few months. A few weeks. So he could have had just a bit of carefree time after Rindi got back.

'Apparently,' said Mum, 'I've been pregnant for three months without knowing it.'

Angus stared at her. Why? Why did he have to get the most stupid, incompetent, hopeless mother on the whole planet?

'How?' he yelled. 'How can you be pregnant for three months without knowing it?'

'Because,' she said, 'the writers didn't tell me.'

Angus felt his mouth drop open.

'They only thought of the idea last week,' said Mum. 'A baby to boost the November ratings. I'd warned them I wasn't going to have any more kids on that show, but as usual they didn't listen. So I'm out of there. I'll have to do a few more weeks taping so they can write me out, then I'm gone.'

Angus gasped for breath. His head hurt. He looked around miserably at the furniture they'd soon have to sell, at the house they'd soon be thrown out of.

He imagined breaking the news to poor Leo and Imogen.

'Mum,' he begged. 'Don't do it. Don't leave. We need the money.'

Mum looked at him. Then she smiled. 'No we don't, silly,' she said. 'I've saved up heaps. We'll never be short of money.'

Angus stared at her, head spinning.

Saved up heaps?

Never be short of money?

Angus struggled to take it all in.

Mum's brow crinkled with concern. 'Look at you,' she said. 'So stressed.' She gave Angus a hug. Angus felt relief flooding through him.

It was all going to be OK.

Now she'd saved up lots of money, Mum could afford to start being a mum.

'I've been thinking since the school play,' said Mum quietly. 'I've been thinking that me and Dad have never really appreciated exactly what and who you are. I've decided to do something about that.'

Angus felt like he was going to faint with happiness.

He didn't care.

Mum seemed to be doing a pretty good job of holding him.

'It's your birthday next week,' said Mum. 'I'm going to have a birthday dinner for you. I'm going to invite your dad and Leo's dad and Imogen's dad so we can all thank you for being the most grown-up, responsible, dependable twelve-year-old in Australia.'

Angus sat up and stared at her.

His insides started to sink.

'I'll be depending on you even more from now on,' said Mum, 'because the network has given me a new series. It's a sit-com about a woman who desperately wants kids but can't get pregnant. Isn't it exciting? I've always wanted to do a sit-com. I've always wanted to bring laughter and happiness to people.'

Angus tried to speak but he couldn't.

He was dumb with disappointment.

'I know,' said Mum. 'I was speechless too when they told me. It'll mean me working slightly longer hours, but I know I can rely on you, my Mr Dependable.'

She hugged him again.

Angus didn't stop her. He was too weak with despair.

And too busy thinking hard.

'Now,' said Mum, rubbing her hands, 'here's the exciting part. The network wants a photo shoot of me and my family. You know, to publicise me leaving the old series and starting the new one. So we're going to have your birthday dinner in the studio and have all the photographers there. You don't have to be nervous because I'll tell you what to do on the night.'

Angus felt his insides start to lurch and shudder like a submarine struggling to the surface.

Suddenly he knew what had to be done.

But was he brave enough?

He waited for his heart to stop racing.

Then he looked directly at Mum.

'Don't worry, Mum,' he said. 'I know exactly what to do.'

23

Angus stood on the lighting walkway and watched all the activity on the studio floor below.

People were scurrying around Mum's spotless TV dining room putting the finishing touches to the dining table. Photographers were testing their flashes. Journalists were interviewing Mum.

Dad, Number Two and Number Three were already seated at the table, hungrily eyeing the oysters and sushi.

Angus felt Leo shiver next to him.

'Do you like raw fish?' asked Leo, peering down.

'No,' said Angus, 'I don't.'

'Yukky,' murmured Imogen.

Angus saw that down below they were almost ready to start. 'Where's Angus?' he heard Mum say.

Suddenly his new suit felt tight and uncomfortable. He took the jacket off and wished he could take the trousers off too, but of course he couldn't.

He needed what was in the pockets.

'We like mashed potato and pumpkin best, don't we?' said Leo.

'Yes,' said Angus, 'we do.'

'Yummy,' gurgled Imogen.

Angus heard something. He looked along the walkway and saw a figure coming towards them. For a panicked second he thought it was a security guard.

It wasn't. It was Rindi.

Angus glowed with pleasure.

'Welcome back,' he said.

'G'day,' she grinned. 'Glad I got here in time.'

They smiled at each other for a long moment, then she handed him the Bumface jacket.

'Thanks,' he said.

He put it on.

'Suits you,' smiled Rindi and gave his arm a squeeze.

Angus saw that her eyes were shining, and he knew it wasn't just her excitement at what he was about to do.

He took a deep breath. Then he gripped the rope he'd tied to the lighting gantry above the centre of the studio, climbed up onto the handrail, and jumped.

As he swung high over his birthday dinner, he gave a loud pirate yell and his insides tingled with the joy of it.

'Bumface,' he heard Rindi and Leo and Imogen yelling delightedly.

Down below, every face looked up, every mouth open.

Mum and Dad weren't watery and indistinct this time. Angus could see every detail of their stunned, shocked, concerned faces.

'Angus,' screamed Mum. 'Be careful.'

'Don't let go,' shouted Dad. 'I'll climb up and get you.'

'The kid's mad,' said Number Three.

'Jeez, Angus,' shouted Number Two, scowling. 'Grow up.'

'No,' yelled Angus.

Not yet, he thought, reaching into his pocket for a handful of mashed potato and pumpkin.

He flung it at them joyfully.

Not yet.

The Other Facts of Life

by Morris Gleitzman

Ben is behaving very strangely.

He's been shutting himself in the bathroom every day for two weeks. His parents are worried. Is it time they told him about THE FACTS OF LIFE?

But Ben actually has some other questions he needs to ask. Whatever it takes, he's determined to get some answers. And so begins a crusade that's both deadly serious – and very, very funny.

Second Childhood

by Morris Gleitzman

Mark's father has always wanted him to be a Somebody. But unless Mark picks up at school, it looks like he's heading down the wrong track. Until . . . Mark and his friends discover they've lived before. Not only that – they were Famous and Important People!

But then they find out they've been responsible for several of the world's big problems. So Henry Ford, Queen Victoria, Albert Einstein and even a famous racehorse get together to see if they can make up for their terrible mistakes . . .

Two Weeks With the Queen

by Morris Gleitzman

'I need to see the Queen about my sick brother.'

Colin Mudford is on a quest. His brother Luke has cancer and the doctors in Australia don't seem able to cure him. Sent to London to stay with his Aunty Iris, Colin reckons it's up to him to find the best doctor in the world.

And how better to do this than by asking the Queen to help . . .

'One of the best books I've ever read. I wish I had written it' – Paula Danziger

Read more in Puffin

For complete information about books available from Puffin – and Penguin – and how to
order them, contact us at the appropriate address below. Please note that for copyright
reasons the selection of books varies from country to country.

www.puffin.co.uk

In the United Kingdom: Please write to Dept EP, Penguin Books Ltd,
Bath Road, Harmondsworth, West Drayton, Middlesex UB7 ODA

In the United States: Please write to Penguin Putnam Inc., P.O. Box 12289,
Dept B, Newark, New Jersey 07101–5289 or call 1–800–788–6262

In Canada: Please write to Penguin Books Canada Ltd,
10 Alcorn Avenue, Suite 300, Toronto, Ontario M4V 3B2

In Australia: Please write to Penguin Books Australia Ltd,
P.O. Box 257, Ringwood, Victoria 3134

In New Zealand: Please write to Penguin Books (NZ) Ltd,
Private Bag 102902, North Shore Mail Centre, Auckland 10

In India: Please write to Penguin Books India Pvt Ltd,
11 Panscheel Shopping Centre, Panscheel Park, New Delhi 110 017

In the Netherlands: Please write to Penguin Books Netherlands bv,
Postbus 3507, NL–1001 AH Amsterdam

In Germany: Please write to Penguin Books Deutschland GmbH,
Metzlerstrasse 26, 60594 Frankfurt am Main

In Spain: Please write to Penguin Books S. A., Bravo Murillo 19,
1° B, 28015 Madrid

In Italy: Please write to Penguin Italia s.r.l.,
Via Felice Casati 20, I–20124 Milano

In France: Please write to Penguin France S. A.,
17 rue Lejeune, F–31000 Toulouse

In Japan: Please write to Penguin Books Japan, Ishikiribashi Building,
2–5–4, Suido, Bunkyo-ku, Tokyo 112

In South Africa: Please write to Longman Penguin Southern Africa (Pty) Ltd,
Private Bag X08, Bertsham 2013